The Training of the Disciples

This edition published 2026
by Living Book Press

ISBN: 978-1-76153-828-5 (hardcover)
         978-1-76153-887-2 (softcover)

First published in 1914.

A catalogue record for this book is available from the National Library of Australia

The Saviour of the World

Book 6

The Training of the Disciples

by

CHARLOTTE M. MASON

LIVING BOOK PRESS

Dominus et Magister (Lord and Master)
(4th Century Mosaic. Detail. Central Figure).
See Appendix I.

Contents

DEDICATION

TO

THE REV. W. H. DRAPER, M.A.

A HEEDLESS traveller stumbled at a stile,
And one came by who stretched a friendly hand
To help o'er treach'rous places in a land
Where joyous trod the traveller mile by mile.

To aid a halting "foot," to reconcile
A rebel "accent" with the general scheme,
To seize each subtle nuance in the theme
And greet a fit word with the happy smile
Of one to whom fit words afford delight-
(Things of the Spirit dearer in his sight),-

E'en thus, accomplish'd Friend, did you beguile
Slack hands to utmost labour: "Leave the rest;
This task is worth it; pray you, give your best !"--

Urged you the laggard on with godly wile!
Wherefore with gratitude I dedicate
To you this little book with theme so great.

C. M. M.

Preface

"Both in philosophy and religion, the μαθητής is a distinct character, and Charles Marriot was an example of it at its best. He had its manly and reasonable humility, its generous trustfulness, its self-forgetfulness; he had, too, the enthusiasm of loving and recognising a great master and teacher, and doing what he wanted done; and he learned from the love of his master to love what he believed truth still more. The character of a disciple does not save a man from difficulties, from trouble and perplexity; but it tends to save him from idols of his own making. It is something, in the trials of life and faith, to have a consciousness of knowing or having known some one greater and better and wiser than oneself, of having felt the spell of his guidance and example."

I have ventured to quote Dean Church's exposition of the relation of a master to a disciple to a human master, (the Rev. Charles Marriot to Dr. Pusey's)[1] because a chief object of this volume is, and indeed, of the work of which it is a part, is to emphasize and define the status of a disciple *quâ* disciple in such ways as a reverent following of the text allows.

We are perhaps a little apt to sum up that which we owe as Christians under the headings of faith, love, and good works, failing to give devout consideration to the Teaching Office of *Magister*, the studious habit due from *Discipline*.

---

[1] The History of the Oxford Movement.

Sometimes we forget to consider what behooves us as scholars to whom is set the task of learning to understand and apply the Unique Philosophy in-cluded in the Christian Religion. It is earnest and devout endeavour—of any age, of all sorts and conditions—who set themselves to form a vivid conception of the Life among men, and labour to understand the Teaching of our Lord and Saviour Jesus Christ. I would venture to hope that this little volume may be acceptable. May I once again acknowledge my indebtedness to the Rev. C. James, the Chronologist writer of whose *Gospel History* I have followed throughout.

C. M. M.

CONTENTS OF VOLUME I
THE HOLY INFANCY

Angels and prophets long had searched in vain
Those mysteries, now, for wayfarers writ plain:

How Christ was born in Bethlehem of pure Maid,
How to three kings His Rising was displayed;

How holy Simeon blessed Him and foretold
His Mother's grief, He, sacrificed and sold.

How out of Egypt did God call His Son
That all the prophets figured might be done.

How, simple Child, He dwelt in Galilee
That simple folk His light might daily see.

How to Jerusalem in His twelfth year
He went, before Jehovah to appear:

How there He shed His light, a duteous Boy,
To keep the law His errand, not destroy.

How eighteen years of meek submission then
Prepared Him for His labours amongst men.

How He went out to John to be baptised,
And John in Him a greater recognised.

How in the wilderness for Forty Days
He bare assaults of Satan. Give we praise!

How in Cana He made the water wine,
That men should see of life in Him a sign.

How in Jerusalem quick drew He forth
The traders and their wares—of how small worth!

How journeying north to Galilee once more,
He sate and taught that Woman heavenly lore.

How all the men came out who heard His fame,
And, Saviour of the World, did Him proclaim.

These things have we considered as we might,
And hence would meekly follow in His light.

CONTENTS OF VOLUME II
HIS DOMINION

CHRIST healed the rich man's son; the man believed;
"God is a spirit," the lesson he received.

He preaches to His own; mad hate they bring,—
Would from steep brow of hill the Saviour fling!

People who sat in darkness saw great light
Whose brightness baffled unaccustomed sight;

Those fishers four on Sea of Galilee
The fishers of the Lord were called to be:

At Capernaum Christ preached; the people heard,
And knew Authority was in His word.

Vile spirit bade He forth in that same hour,
And all men recognised an unknown Power.

Peter's wife's mother, raised from fevered bed—
By hand that raised her would thenceforth be led.

"At even ere the sun was set," they came
To Him for healing, sick and blind and lame.

Then wearied, He, a great while before day,
Went out to desert place that He might pray.

The folk of Galilee would make Him King;
He knows how little worth the praise they bring.

Weary with preaching, Christ bade put to sea;—
Behold, a wondrous draught, the fishers' fee!

A leper cried, Thou canst,—wilt make me clean?
I will, saith Christ; healed, who had leprous been!

Levi took customs' dues by the seaside,
And when the Master called, he straight replied.

His Jews rejected for hypocrisy;
Too skilled in subterfuge, what hope have we?

Man at Bethesda's pool so long had lain—
The Lord who healed him to betray was fain!

Christ taught,—the Father and the Son were One
In words They spake, in all works They had done.

On the Son the royal crown of judgment set;—
He learned the ways of men, nor would forget:

In Him was Life; and all the souls that live
Draw breath from Him, to Him their praises give.

The Law, the prophets, witness; to each heart,
The Father testifies, and shows his part.

Thy Jews condemned, grant us, good Lord, to heed—
Unstable in our faith, slack in our deed!

Christ walked in cornfield on the Sabbath day,
And set men free from bondage whilst they pray.

He instantly the withered hand restores,
And, grieved, the Rulers' faithlessness deplores.

Once more to fair Gennesareth He came,
And multitudes drew nigh, with love aflame.

Our Founder chose the Twelve, and laid them, sure
Stones to sustain that Church which shall endure.

He charged them; told them, how the poor are blest;
How persecutions should their lives molest:

Taught them the brother-secret; how to give;
How with all men as brothers they should live.

Of blind man led by blind man, cupboard's store,
Of building House of Faith, He told them more:

And then He climbed the Mount that all might hear,—
That multitude had come from far and near:

"Blessed are they that mourn," He told the sad;—
With promise of the Father's care made glad.

Chaste must they be and kind and guard their speech;—
For God's own holiness is in man's reach.

He taught men how to give their alms, to pray;
And all their anxious fears to put away.

Behold, the Church He founded on that day
Received those Institutes should guide her Way.

The people heard, and hardly understood,
But knew the Word He spake was very good;

Perceived Authority in every word
And fain would bear due fruit of that they'd heard.

CONTENTS OF VOLUME III
THE KINGDOM OF HEAVEN

*The centurion, begging that the Lord would heal
His suffering servant, did great faith reveal.*

*Behold, with joy return the mourning train
Come forth to bury that young man of Nain.*

*The prisoner, John, makes question by his friends;
News of His works, the answer Jesus sends.*

*"What went ye to the wilderness to see?"
Cried Jesus, praising John's fidelity.*

*A woman anoints His feet with costly nard;
Christians shall know thy deed—her great reward.*

*He walks in Galilee, and women tend,
And gladly of their substance on Him spend.*

*The sower sowed in various kinds of ground;
The Lord to hearts of men a likeness found.*

Who knows the things of God and doth not tell,
Like him who hides a lamp, doth not do well.

Together are let grow the wheat and tares,
Till each kind to its place the reaper bears.

Thou think'st to watch the growing of the seed?
A secret, that,—so by God's will decreed.

A grain of mustard-seed, so small to see,
May yet become a mighty sheltering tree.

Thou'st found a treasure? Go and sell thine all,
Ere thou this treasure all thine own may'st call.

The woman hid the leaven in her flour;
The Word hid in a heart shall rise with power.

A merchant came upon a pearl of price
And forthwith bought—by liberal device.

And, "Have ye understood?" the Saviour cried;
"Yea, Lord," they said, but in their lives denied.

"Thy mother and Thy brethren would Thee see;"
"These be My kinsfolk—they who follow Me."

Proud Nazareth rejected Him who came
To save the humble; Do not we the same?

Jesus came walking o'er the stormy sea;
His friends, relieved, were there—where they would be.

The demoniac raged as fierce as angry storm;
Christ spake,—and meek he sat who'd wrought such
    harm.

The little maid was raised by Jesus' hand:
"Now, see ye no man tell," the Lord's command.

A woman crept behind and healing took;
Christ made her happy by a pitying look.

Two blind men came and cried on Him for sight;
The Lord restored to these the joys of light.

A dumb deaf man sat moody by the way;—
Christ taught dumb lips to praise His name that day.

The time had come to send the Twelve abroad,—
Bless'd messengers to carry forth the Word.

As father charges son would cross the seas,
So Christ, their Father, gave His charge to these.

"Dangers I see await you on your way;—
Be prudent, friends, and bide a better day.

But have no fear; knows not your Father all
Of good or ill His children shall befall?

Yet ye must bear the cross, nor shrink in shame
From any obloquy or any blame.

Of this be sure, whoever you befriends,
Your Father in heaven will make that man amends."

Forth fared the Twelve in pairs to do His will,
And as they went, the Lord was with them still.

With joy these men returned to shew their Lord
How it had prospered with the seed, His Word.

Now, John the Baptist prisoned in strong tower
To chide the king had used a prophet's power:

The king sware foolish oath to grant what boon
The princess asked of him; vindictive, soon—

"Give me John Baptist's head," she cried; and, lo,
The sorry king bade armed men to go

And bring the prophet's head. The news was brought
To John's disciples; quick they Jesus sought

And told their grief to Him. "Come ye apart,"
Saith Christ to the weary Twelve; with tender heart

They follow Him and tell what things befell
In all the cities—whether ill or well.

CONTENTS OF VOLUME IV
THE BREAD OF LIFE

"Come ye apart into a desert place;"
But, quick the folk the Master's steps to trace:

All day the Master spake; the people heard,
And hungered while they listened to the Word.

"Give them to eat," He said: and one produced
A meal scarce more than one to eat was used.

Christ blessed and gave to all that multitude
And all were filled with meat—and gratitude.

He bade His friends take ship; then sent away
The folk, and climbed the mountain there to pray.

A storm arose; He looked and saw them row
Their little craft while wild the winds did blow.

He walks upon the sea; they take Him in;
Instant, subsides the tempest's fearful din.

Next day the people seek Him in the place
Where He had fed them amply by His grace.

Returned, they question Him; and mysteries,—
The work of God, the bread of God,—to these

Unlearned He discloses; shows them how
God gave the manna as He feeds men now.

Having made plain that life-sustaining bread
Must ever come from God, He turned and said,—

"I am the bread of life; who eats of Me,
That man alone eternal life shall see."

His disciples were offended: "How can He
Give us His flesh to eat? Can such thing be?"

Many forsook Him and fled; the Lord was grieved:
"Will ye, too, go away?" they who believed

Were asked in sadness: one stood up and said,—
"Thou hast the words by which a man is led

"In the ways of life; to whom then should we go?"
Peter, that happy saint who answered so.

"Nay, you Twelve have I chosen, and one of you
Is a devil:" said the Lord, whose word is true.

❧

He told of things which most defile a man;
Not casual soil, but evil which he can

Conceal in his heart while outwardly he's clean;
But his foul secret thoughts by God are seen.

Nor shall one unto God that portion give
Which he owes to his father—that the man may live.

He journeyed northwards to the coasts of Tyre;
A woman came with passionate desire

That He would heal her daughter, sorely vexed;
Nor at His chiding did she go perplexed,

But spake that word of faith the Lord approved,
And He healed the little daughter whom she loved.—

"The dogs," she said, "the crumbs that fall may eat,"
And Christ received her at His mercy-seat.

A dumb-deaf man they brought; He touched his tongue;
"He hath done all things well!"—the people sung.

Again, a desert place the Saviour sought;
The people followed and their sick folk brought.

Three days they listened to the Master's Word;
Ah, blessed folk who on the mountain heard!

Once more He fed them from a trifling store;
They ate till none was willing to eat more.

Before and after that great word of BREAD
Which He is, the Lord the hungry people fed;

That none might say, "Such Bread's a thing of nought;"—
Unlike the daily bread men ate and bought.

CHRIST and the Twelve land at the sunset hour;
Men ask a sign to manifest His power.

The sign of Jonas,—is the Lord's reply;
From those unfriendly shores with haste they fly.

"Beware of the leaven of the Pharisees,"
He bids the Twelve; and they their Lord would please,

And chide themselves that they had not brought bread.
Enough in the boat for each man to be fed.

The blind man of Bethsaida they brought
To Christ, who took his hand and led him out

Apart from the rest; cured him in stages three,—
In each of which a parable we see.

They journey north,—a pilgrimage oppressed
With coming woe—towards Hermon's snowy crest;

And, on the way, foretelling grief and loss,
He bids the Twelve go forth and bear the cross.

"He that will save his life, that life shall lose;
He saves his life who doth not death refuse."

And now He takes the three and climbs the mount
With heavy steps the weary men scarce count.

The Lord knelt down and prayed; the Twelve went, sleep,
Too weary loving watch with Him to keep.

They waked, and, lo, the Lord was seated there,
Shining and glorious—most exceeding fair!

And two spake with Him, men of royal mien;—
Persons so noble no man yet had seen:—

Moses and Elias, come to cheer the Lord,
Before His coming conflict, with the Word

Writ in the Scriptures for Him to fulfil,—
Accomplishing in all the Father's will.

A sudden cloud enwrapped the glorious sight,
And the three, scarce sensible for joy and fright.

As they descend the mountain, lo, a crowd,—
A wretched father cries on Him aloud

To save his son, possessed; Christ drew them out,
The demons who had brought this ill about.

They left that region, sore oppressed with grief;
For Christ had brought home to their slow belief

The great things He must suffer, and the pains
They too should bear,—full gladly for all those gains

They found in Jesus and the words He taught:
Now, tardy steps the heavy pilgrims brought

To the house of Peter, there, in Galilee,—
Capernaum, fair city by the sea.

One came to Peter for his temple dues;
"Half shekel, too, your Lord will not refuse."

"Go to Gennesareth and cast a hook;
Draw the first fish to land, nor pause to look:"

He went, and in its mouth a shekel found,
And paid those dues on every man were bound.

When all were in the house, now hear Him say,—
"What matter, then, discuss'd ye by the way?"

They were ashamed, for, Who should be the first,
Was their dispute; and none of them now durst

Confess his fault: Christ took a little child,
And looking round with loving aspect mild;—

"Look on this child; humble yourselves as he;—
Behold, the greatest in the kingdom, ye!"

Of peace, of salt, of many things He spake;
Of certain woe should that man overtake

Who scorned the little children, hindered those
Whom the Lord cherishes because He knows.

And as a limner draws stroke here and there,
And every stroke reveals the aspect fair

Of him the painter limns, so these perceived
The grace of Him in whom they had believed

Produced in clearer outline by each word
Which sorrowful, yet glad, they meekly heard.

CONTENTS OF VOLUME V
THE GREAT CONTROVERSY

Of forgiveness, spake the Lord to angry men
Who, hurt, conceived that they might hurt again!

"Till seven time seventy shall thy brother sin,
And thou with love endeavour him to win.

And then the Lord told tale of him, abused
His master's kindness and his wealth misused;

And when his Lord forgave him all that debt,
His own poor debtor's plea with harshness met.

Ah, blessed country, how thy paths are dear!
Christ walked in Galilee when Death was near.

His brethren, unbelieving, urged that He
Should in Jerusalem work, that all might see.

He went not up with them their joy to share,
But, later, went, "in secret as it were."

In Jerusalem, behold, a wondrous throng,
All come for sacrifice and holy song.

They talk and wonder much, "Will Jesus come?"
"Here hath He enemies: He'll bide at home!"

Christ to the Temple came and people taught
The learned wondering whence His lore He brought.

He tells them, None shall know but he who wills;
And great astonishment those doctors fills.

That they intend to kill Him, Christ perceives;
But, of the strangers, none this thing believes.

"A devil hath he!" country people cry;
Christ bids them not condemn Him ere they try.

The townsfolk know their rulers' wicked plot,
Yet would not have their alms and zeal forgot.

They know Him and His kinsfolk, they declare;
Christ shews, there's more to know than they're aware.

He offered them the truth, and bade them choose,
Would they believe His word or dare refuse?

They feared when told that He would go away:
"Nay, whither goes He? Where, then can he stay?"

For all their proud derision, in their heart,
They knew the Christ full surely would depart.

The prophet, dry of soul and much distress'd,
Saw that fair stream which all the nations bless'd.

Christ stood and cried,--Come unto Me and drink
Ye fainting souls who on life's highway sink!

The thirsting people heard and would obey;
But Nature cried, There is an easier way!

One more hard saying, powerful to divide,
The people found those words that Jesus cried.

The Sanhedrin send officers to take;
They touch not Christ, for, "Never man so spake!"

A shameful woman to the Lord they bring;
He bids the innocent the first stone fling.

The people sat in darkness; none could tell
Which way to go, or choose 'twixt ill and well.

Then ONE stood up and cried, I AM THE LIGHT!
And sudden vision cheered their darkened sight.

"I know when I came forth, and whither go:"
These be two things no man may ever know.

Who art Thou?" ask they, though the Lord had told,
And they mocked His words, --in ignorance, bold.

"I have many things to judge concerning you;"
They flinch before the Judge who all things knew.

"As Abram rose, obedient unto Me,
I bid you quit the ways where sinners be!"

"Who followeth Me, lo, he shall never die."
"Dead long ago do all our fathers lie!"

"I seek not Mine own honour," spake the Lord;
But they, vainglorious, mocked at His meek word.

"Abraham was glad, for he My day beheld!
How hast Thou, not yet old, seen men of eld?"

"Before Abraham was I AM, "the Lord declared:
Thus, all the ages have the Saviour shared.

❦

The disciples moved with pity, asked the Lord,
"Has this man sinned, that he's from sight debarr'd?!

"Nay, suffering may become a work divine,
Enduring much, make ye God's glory shine."

Then to the man,--"Go, wash in Siloam's pool."
His blindness left him at the waters cool.

Saith Christ,--"Dost on the Son of God believe?"
"Lord, knew I Him, how glad would I receive!"

"That, whereas I was blind, now do I see,--"
The blind man's evidence serves you and me.

❦

The silly sheep Christ gathers in His fold,
Where we may enter free nor be too bold.

When the Good Shepherd calls, with answering bleat,
His sheep come flocking close about His feet

The sheep are safely herded in the fold;
The Shepherd seeks out wanderers in the cold.

The sheep, they be but silly go astray
At every turning in the narrow way:

They wander into every hazardous place;
The careful Shepherd doth the wanderers trace.

Again Christ to Jerusalem returns,
And there more fiercely hate against Him burns.

Eternal Life He offers to His own;
And, full of wrath, the Jews the Lord would stone.

Christ hid Himself from those so violent men
By quiet Pool, where many sought Him then.

There came a message from a household dear;
"Lazarus is sick; we know Thou wilt draw near!"

Three days He tarried; then said, Let us go;
Lazarus is dead; but ye shall mysteries know.

He goes; the sisters meet Him and complain,
Had He been there Lazarus had not been ta'en.

He shews what Resurrection signifies,
They think,--"What hope for us since Lazarus dies?"

"Lazarus, come forth!" is the Almighty word;
The dead man came and stood before his Lord!

BOOK I

The Disciples in Training

Should one rise from the dead,—
The Lord Himself hath said,—
It were of no avail,
Men's doubts would still prevail:
So, men saw Lazarus rise
Nor yet believed their eyes!

I

Some tell the Pharisees

As when a morn of light is drowned in gloom,
The wind veers west towards the bitter north,
The rain is edged with ice, the snow falls thick,
And men's hearts fail them for the lack of cheer,—
So was it with those mourners round the tomb
Whence Lazarus came forth. They'd seen the whole;
They saw what cloud of Death whose heavy shade
Weighs down the lives of men lift up and roll
From the face of heaven, letting forth the light:
Hope was revealed; they thought they surely knew
What 'twas to hope; longing for this or that,
How many times they'd feared, yet hoped for good:
But, now, HOPE rose transcendent as a god,
Compelling and fulfilling. But what art
Could show that radiant form or who portray;
Or shape in words the Resurrection joy?
A-tiptoe as for flight, the group stood round,
Each face illumined with the light of Hope,
A new conception, not yet brought to birth.
Then fell that sudden pall: a blast of doubt.
From hearts a-cold blew chilling on all souls:
Those, unbelieving, told the Pharisees:
What was't to them, Shadow of Death withdrawn?

GAINSBOROUGH (AFTER REMBRANDT)

"What Do We? For This Man
Doeth Many Miracles."

II

"What do we?"

Now Panic, imp let loose from hell to scare
Sound judgment, reason, duty, from the breasts
Of men who careless let the mischief in
And pass it to their neighbours, keeping, still,
The fear they give away, —wild Panic seized
These sober men, the Pharisees and priests.
Here, sooth, a sign done before all men's eyes,—
Th' raising of Lazarus, man of good repute:
In temple courts and streets, men stood in groups;
Distraught and whisp'ring, they discussed the news:
Here was a crisis which some action asked,
Immediate, before the Council sate
In ordered state to judge by Israel's laws;
So hasty summons called the Seventy,
Who met disordered in their stately hall
As though invaders sat before their gates.

Spake one, "What do we, then: Why sit we still
And let this man as thief come in the night
Make spoil of Israel's heart? Idle we watch,
Dally in philosophic mood supine,

Think to confound Him with neat syllogisms,—
He turns Him round and with one measured word,
O'erthrows us where we're strongest."
  A Second. Thou hast said;
As imbeciles we dally with our fate!
Whilst we discuss, with laboured argument
Would disprove this and that He spake, one word
From Him, and, lo, our truth's a lie; divest
Of faith and hope, we naked stand. IF we,
The Jews, set to maintain, the Law, fence round
High ordinance, keep worship pure for men,
If we betray our trust at this Man's word,
Cease to believe our Calling, in the Law,
Tradition of the elders, nay, God's choice
Of Israel for His own,—what, then, of them,
The common people, easily gulled?
  A Third. They'll go;
Public opinion surges under us,
We stagger where we stand: no common risk
We run if we allow this Man to live;
"Tis we or He! In Judah is no room
For two so opposed as are we Scribes and He.
But let Him be, and, ere the fifth moon wax,
All men shall do His bidding; what of us?
  A Fourth. Ye count without the Romans, what
    think they?
As 'tis, we're let be for we have no Head;
No voice amongst us sways the people's heart
To turn it hither, thither; inchoate,
As shifting dust in wind, they hold our race,—

No nation, but a horde, men hardly held
By any common bond—what hurt work we
Against the Empire, knit by law and zeal?
But leave the people free to make Him King,
And Rome gets up—a sleeping lion roused
And tears us in her wrath!
                        Then stood up one,
High priest for that same year, with eye entranced,
And that afflatus which Elijah, once,
And all the prophets felt who spake God's word:—
    Caiaphas. Nothing ye know, nor, in your cautious
        schemes,
Take count of how, it is expedient
Aye, in the eyes of God, that one should die
For the people that the nation perish not!
What means the law of sacrifice to you—
Is't not that one should die that all be saved?
'A lamb,' ye say, 'but what of that?' Ye fools,
Poor ignorant! The lamb is but the sign,
Symbol of truth, that God would have one die,
A man, to save his nation! Out on you,
Cowards and slow of heart!

                 Aye, one should die,—
But not for th' Jews alone that Sacrifice
Consummate; but for tardy hearts, blind souls
That vaguely stretch to touch the Infinite;
For all men know, though taught of none, a God,
Quite other than their augurs, medicine men
Portray—God, to delight men's souls, fulfil,

Save, govern, to Himself draw heavy hearts;
Yea, all men should the Sacrifice redeem
And gather into one: while Caiaphas
Imagined 'twas his shift to save the Jews,
Nor knew, the purposes of God, how deep!
So from that hour the Jews laid wait for Him.

III

He tarried at Ephraim

OH, happy Ephraim, bordering on the waste!
Right royal city hast thou, sudden, grown!
What though thy walls enclose but little space,
Thy battlements have meagre wealth to guard,—
An hour of rich fulfilment comes to thee!
Dost know, thou little city amongst hills,
The KING'S within thy walls, the King of Kings!
What, ho, ye watchmen, be alert on guard!
Fly Judah's royal pennon from your towers,
Hang broideries by all your common ways,
Lay costly carpets in your sordid streets,
Array you, sons of Ephraim, be glad!
For who are ye to have the King with you,
The King and His twelve peers?
                Not so the Christ
Visits the haunts of men; no blazonry
Of heralds, trumpets' blare, proclaim the news
That a Great One has arrived. Scarce any turned
To watch the meek procession of the Lamb

That day He brought His twelve to hide them there,
In this sequestered city of small note;
The Light of the World was there and needs must
    shine;
Blest men of Ephraim who saw the Light!

SANDRO BOTTICELLI

Fortitude.
"O Fortitude Divine!"

IV

He set His face to go to Jerusalem

As happy schoolboy marks off, day by day,
The days must pass ere, lessons o'er, he flies
To home and love and all upgathered joys,—
So Christ kept calendar, a secret score;—
None other knew He should be taken up,
And none perceived the anguish of the way,
The Dolorous Way, He trod; though all was writ
A thousand years before for men to read,—
How Christ should go as Lamb to slaughter led;
The smiting and the scorn, the Judgment Halls
Where He should stand accused nor open mouth,
Dumb as sheep led to slaughter; vile offence,
To read whereof, we beat our breasts and cry,
For we are men, and men have done this thing!

Those days were well-nigh come, and, knowing it,
Christ set His face towards Jerusalem!
O, Fortitude Divine, that, seeing all
As 'twere in mirror shewn,—each act of shame
Wrought on Him, every awful grief endured,—
He waited not their will, those murderous Jews,

But went to th' Death whose poignancy He knew,
And all attendant shames; "It cannot be,"
Saith Christ, "that prophet perish out of thee,
Jerusalem, who hast the prophets slain!"

As one bound on a painful pilgrimage
Counts o'er the joys of home, seeks every room,
And handles this and that, the things he loved,
For remembrance, ere he goes, so did the Lord
Seek Galilee again to take fond leave
Of lake-side haunts, sweet dales, of humble roofs
Had sheltered the Son of Man?

V

The Samaritan Village

Not wholly without state Messias went
On this last progress to His capital:
Messengers ran to seek place for the Church,—
The Lord and His twelve friends.
                    The Passover
Was night, and multitudes with faces set
Towards Jerusalem filled the ways; so when these
    came
To buy bread, hire chamber, the villagers
With fury set on them and drave them thence!
Men should behave with modest deference
Who visit foreign places; had these erred?
Nay, but Samaria would have none of them,—
Journeying towards Jerusalem; for old
Animosity moved every peasant's breast.

See we the Lord, austere and merciful,
Turn to regard the inhospitable crew;
A look convicted them of shameful act,
A glance to haunt and grieve in days to come.
But James and John were of another mind—

40

Those Sons of Thunder! "Lord, shall we call down
The lightning to consume these haughty men,
E'en as Elijah did? Thou'rt great as he,
Thou, too, commandest heaven's artillery,
Let their offence be punished!"
                    But the Lord
Spake grievous word: "Have ye been with Me, then,
These many months, these years, nor learned ye
        aught?
Can ye discern the spirits, whose they be,
That urge, compel, a man? Perceive ye not
Whence murderous anger comes, o'erwhelming hate?
A child conning his lessons knows these things,
Else, how guides he his life? Ye teach him first
That gentle motions from God's Spirit flow;
That anger, wrath, all sullen hate, from him—
The murderer from the beginning. Go,
Get ye the lesson set you on that day
When Peter asked, How oft? Not yet know ye
What spirit ye are of."
                    Then James and John
Perceived, abashed, how great their hasty fault;
The Samaritan's offence was not for them
To judge: of hostile spirit were those men,
Hating and hateful? See, a curtain raised
In th' inmost chamber of each saint revealed
A heart of murderous wrath! The holy two
Would fain excuse them, "Twas for Jesus' sake!"
But HE will none on't—that excuse, nor dare
The men ope lips to voice the futile plea.

Thenceforth and evermore they knew this thing;—
Two spirits wait to dominate each man;
One of the twain shall rule; the choice is his;
Would he, malicious, hurt and hate a man
For any wrong to him or them he loves?
All hate, all black resentment's sudden flood,
O'erwhelming, from one spirit emanates,
The guest solicited of envious hearts.
Would he, benevolent, forgive the wrong
And seek to serve that other wronging him
The man hath opened to the Spirit of God
Who cometh as a fertilizing flood
And fills his heart with overflowing peace!

VI

I have transgressed
(The Disciple)

AH, Lord, I have transgressed! hot words I spake
In wrath against my fellow, nor would take
His word that he repented!

Ah, Lord, I have transgressed! resentment burned
Within me, for I was unduly spurned;
Nor knew that I resented!

Ah, Lord, I have transgressed! Another praised
Hath sometime shameful envy in me raised—
So mean am I presented!

Ah, Lord, I have transgressed! this time my sin
So pitiless, so hard, it needs must win
Thy rod—that I consented!

Ah, Lord, forgive! till seventy times seven
And seventy times again, exceeding even
Thy measure—covenanted!

So shall I learn perchance those sins to see
With gentler eyes that others do to me,—
Mine own sins, sore lamented!

VII

"I will follow"

Rejected of that village, see them go,
A sorrowful procession, meek and low;
For had not Christ rebuked them?

A man stood by who noted all the scene,—
Rejection, wrath, reproof, with curious mien:
"Not thus do Men behave them!"

Sudden, his heart convinced, he cried and said
"Master, I'll follow whither I be led!"
(Men follow who will lead them.)

Jesus, beholding, knew this generous soul;
Perceived he had not yet discerned the whole
Demand He laid upon them

Who follow Christ: "Foes have holes," said He,
"Birds have their nests; the Son of Man must be
Denied poor things that please them!"

Did th' man go sorrowful for all that good
Of daily ease he scarce had understood?
Privations, could he bear them?

VIII
"Follow Me!"

As, pensive, went the Master on His way,
He met a man whose eye a need confessed;
His history was writ in instant's play
Of glance, revealing that he sought the best,
And in the face of Christ perceived his rest:
The Lord beheld his love, and "Follow Me,"
He spake to bless the man, and also test:
Ah me, that we the holiest should see
And for some near concern careless should let it be!

E'en so this man, who knew and loved the Lord,—
Divided duties kept him from his good;
His heart upleapt within him at the Word;
Alas, he could not follow an he would
For that old man, his father, who withstood
His son's desire to leave him ere he died:
"A man must cherish his own flesh and blood
Nor seek another service in his pride!"
Poor man, he answered no, but sore of heart he sighed.

"Yea," said the Lord, who knows the things that
    grieve
A man perplexed, with argument outworn;
"There be, shall never their home duties leave,
But rise to serve their household morn by morn:
But there be men who shall go forth forlorn,
The burden of the Lord upon them laid:
To others leave those cares that thou hast borne;
Go, preach the word, My son, nor be dismayed;
Thy God, shall He not be that old man's staff and aid?"

IX

Fit for the Kingdom

THE Kingdom closes in while it expands!
For alien peoples and for other lands
Mayhap its bounds shall widen, but, to-day,
How narrow is the entrance, strait the way!

The populous road, where many pilgrims went
Towards Jerusalem on festive thoughts intent,
Affords one party diff'ring from the rest,—
The Twelve who follow Him they have confess'd.

The folk regard that group with curious eye;
And one, averse to let such chance go by
Without some certain word should fix his faith,
Approacheth Christ, and with due reverence saith,—

"Lord, Thou constrain'st me! I would follow Thee,
Would hear and keep Thy words, those wonders see,
Thou workest on Thy way; but let me go
And bid a kind farewell to them I know!"

The Lord beheld him with that Judge's eye
Which doth a man's most secret things espy;
He knew him quick to feel, to act as prompt;
As water, unstable, in just accompt!

This candidate for Heaven found no place;
Of nature slight, unready for the race
Which calls for loins upgirded, what could he
In Kingdom where the violent victors be?

"Who puts his hand, My son, to that great plough
Which furroweth the nations even now,
Yet looks regretful back not fit is he
A steadfast labourer in My fields to be!"

Doth Christ reject? Methought, for all who came
Was a sure welcome, and for each the same!

X

The Seventy are sent forth

"Come ye apart," saith Christ, "to yonder glade;
Consider those commands upon you laid:"
They gathered round Him as the Lord had said:

And, two by two, He sent before His face
Those Seventy, detached to shew His grace,
To carry words from Him to every place;

To cry,—" Prepare the way, the King's at hand!
Now come we in advance at His command,
That ready at His coming ye may stand!"

They'd heard Him teaching men these many days,
They knew His words of wisdom, gracious ways,
Nor need He teach them how to shew His praise:

Teaching in manners did the Lord impart,
Neglecting nought, He shewed the seemly art
Of meet behaviour in house, street, and mart.

49

"My children, see, the fields are thick with corn;
The golden grain stands ready for that morn
When, 'Go ye forth to reap! 'the cry shall warn:

"Plenteous the harvest but the labourers few;
Pray ye the Lord to send good men and true
To gather in the grain while skies are blue!"

XI
The Charge

FOR you, go on your way and have no fear;
As lambs amongst the wolves do ye appear?
Shall not your Shepherd guard you, ever near!

But ye must go in My bame, nor provide
Those things to ease your way another guide
Would bid you carry, lest ye be denied:

Nor shoes nor purse nor wallet are for you;
Your course with naught provided ye pursue
Who would fulfil Mine errand, servants true:

Nor civil salutations shall ye make
Tho' rich and poor pass by their ways to take;
My service brooks no dallying for their sake.

What house ye enter, cry, "Peace to this house!"
Where any son of peace within allows,
Your peace shall rest, a blessing on that house:

But if, like Noah's dove, your gift shall find
No place of rest, be not of troubled mind;
Your peace returns to bless you and to bind:

They make you welcome, bid you take your seat?
Take such things as they offer, gladly eat;
The labourer is worthy of his meat.

But not self-pleasing shall My servant be,
Faring from hose to house quick-eyed to see
Which neighbour gives to guest the best bounty:

If city ye have come to doth receive,
Take heed the men in you no greed perceive;
Eat that is set before you, by their leave:

To them who give to you with liberal hand
Shall ye give healings, teachings; understand,
Ye shall not fail of any just demand:

Go, tell those friendly men the might news,
Shall save who hears, condemn who dares refuse,__
"The Kingdom of God is here—to win or lose!"

Do they reject, go ye into the street
And shake that city's dust from off your feet,—
That they know their offence through symbol meet!

Think you since Sodom fell no city's failed
To hear the call to judgment, nor assailed
God's prophets, whose high message naught availed?

I tell you, yea, full many have transgressed:
But worse for who My messengers molest
Than for contumacious Sodom,—sin possess'd.

XII

Woe unto thee, Chorazin!

Ah, woful cities, upbraided of your Prince,
Chorazin and Bethsaida! "Had they seen,
E'en Tyre and Sidon, those works which have been
Performed within your walls, they had long since

"Repented them in ashes. Howbeit Isay,
Better for those fierce sinners without fear,
Who never heard the words have graced your ear,
Than for you, reprobate, in th' Judgment Day!

"And thou, Capernaum, what dost thou evince
For the high honours have been done to thee?
I tell thee, Sodom had been turned to Me,
Had she been graced as thou, this long while since!"

Then, doth the Lord judge cities? Shall they be,
Corporate, arraigned 'fore Heaven's high Majesty?

54

XIII

The Return of the Seventy

"SEE, Lord, with joy we come," the Seventy cry;—
"The powers of hell sufficient to defy,
    We cast out devils in Thy name,
        Disease bade we to disappear,
        Restored poor souls oppressed with shame,
        Made blind to see, the deaf to hear;
O Lord, our Lord, what might of Thine is this
That Thou has dower'd us with for poor men's bliss!"

And Christ was glad; rejoiced for one rapt hour
In their bold witness to His saving power:
    "I saw, and lo, upon a day,
        That yet shall dawn, did Satan fall'
    Bright, transient, as the lightning's play,
        His glamour doth the world enthrall;
Ye trace the lightning's course by ruin black,
So devastation marks his blighting track,—

"The enemy of men. But there is hope:
Each passing day sets limits to his scope;
  Discern ye not the light aglow?
    The kingdom cometh among men,
  The Father's love finds course to flow
    Towards His hapless sons again:
Who hind'reth men is vanquish'd, overthrown,—
Now shall they turn them to their God alone.

"See you, a battle throngeth all the air,
And in the conflict shall ye 'Seventy' share:
  Go forth with My Authority;
    No deadly thing shall do you harm,
  Pain and distress before you flee,
    No terrors shall your heart alarm;
But not in singular powers abides your joy—
Whose name is writ in heaven meets no annoy."

XIV
"I Thank Thee, O Father!"

THE Lord beheld the Seventy, simple men
To whom He had discoursed of mighty themes;
And, lifting up His eyes, to praise was fain
The righteous Father, Who th' unlearned deems

Worthy to know; the simple heart sincere,
The little child who few things apprehends
But brings discriminating vision clear,—
To such as these the Father condescends.

The Lord, discerning, lifted thankful heart,
Loving the Seventy, that it was God's will
To shew his mysteries where is no art
To darken counsel with man's subtle skill.

So is it still; the Lord's mind who would know,
With a child's heart shall wait for Him to shew.

XV

The ultimate Knowledge
(The Disciple)

Good Lord, we know not, we are ignorant!
    We move through life as blind man in the street;
    Disaster we may any moment meet;
In perils of thick darkness, light we want!

But, an we knew, securely should we go!
    Thou, Lord, canst keep us safe, for Thou dost see,
    And all things are committed unto Thee;—
Cares of the world, slight things that bring us low,

All, all are in Thy hand, the great and small!
    Safely, poor ignorant, we trust in Thee;
    As blind man bravely steps with one can see,
We, led by Thee, dare walk nor fear a fall!

The inmost mystery Thou dost penetrate;
    To Thee the dark is luminous as day;
    The Father's face sheds brightness on that way
In which our world is led in tranquil state.

Despite those restless heaving as of one
    Toss'd on a troubled sea. As in a glass,
    The lineaments of God the Father pass
Before his gaze who looks upon the Son:

The Son the Father knows, and we through Him
    Seeing the face of God shall dwell at ease:
    But what is this? Only the Father sees
The Son, and manifests to vision dim

Of earthly men the glory of that Lord
    Who came to walk with us and shew the Way,
    Turning our darkness to the radiant day
Which emanates eternal from His Word.

Great is the mystery we must attain!
    A twofold knowledge is for man to know:
    Two LIGHTS must each to us the other shew;
That they are ONE, is our eternal gain.

BOOK II

Rest and Service

XVI
Rest
(The Disciple)

A REST remaineth: is then rest so good?
The hope of weariness, a promise sweet
To labouring souls, but wherefore rest in heaven?

Deeper than any thought of man,
Sweeter than any dream of man,
Fuller than any hope of man,
To conceive which hath not entered
Into any heart of man:

As the sunny air to the life of a bird,
As a fair sea to the way of a ship,
As brooding sleep to the life of a babe,
So the infinite, unutterable rest of God
To those blest souls that are upborne thereon.

The rest we plan,
Wherein to lay us down when labours end,
Is other in its kind: in feelings, thoughts,
In burdens left behind, and chief of all,
In the dear Face of God, we place our rest.

But rest, the pure element
That God hath made as He hath made the air,
Encompassing, conditionless and free,
That each blest life, unconscious, lives within,
　　This enters not our thought.

Once in a life, perhaps (nor then to all)—
When in extremest strait a hopeless soul
Lies down beneath its burden,—heaven's gate opes
And that soul for one supernal moment
Is taken in and steeped and bathed in rest.

　　Thus was it once:
A feeble body, and a brain o'er-fraught
With many thoughts and cares; a desolate heart,
Brooding o'er empty places in the earth
Not to be filled again. Life was too much:
The fainting body and more languid soul
Made plaint, for voice too feeble, Lord, how long?

　　And then it came:
The revelation of the infinite,
　　Eternal rest of God.
It came: but how to tell of it!—
As well give features and a form
To sunshine hallow'd 'neath the charm
　　That quiets summer Sabbaths.

It came; but not with words, too worn the heart
For any sound of words, tho' words of Life:
With the sweet comprehending of a touch
That knew and pitied and was strong to help,
E'en so came quieting from the hand of God;
  And the heart lay still
  And ceased from itself;
Nor purpose, prayer, nor penitence was there,
Nor praise nor love found place, but a great rest;

A rest that steeped that soul and bore it up
And circled it and shadow'd; only rest;
  Not knowing, having, being, aught:
Yet life nor love had ever after brought
  So full a draught.

  And as that soul lay still,
For hours perhaps or moments—lo, there came
A writing on the wall of its hid room;
The words appeared,—"As one is comforted,
  Whom comforteth his mother!" So for aye,
That soul doth wot of one good thing prepared
  Of God for them that love Him.

XVII

"Come unto Me"

Come unto Me, ye heavy laden souls,
Striving and crying for the weight ye bear,
For burden of perplexity and care,—
While no man shares, nor any friend consoles.

What ails ye that ye cannot be at rest?
Uneasy as the waves of ocean, rise
Your troubled hearts before the silent skies,
Uncomforted of any, all unblest.

"The thing that I must bear, I bear alone,"
The proud man utters in his misery;
Go to, My son, it is not meant for thee
Or any man to make his peevish moan,

Alone and burdened more than he can bear;
Come unto Me and I will give thee rest!
I know the oppression heavy on thy breast;
Shall I not ease those burthens that I share?

"Come unto Me, all ye that labour and are heavy laden, and I will give you rest."

E'en as an ox is with its fellow yoked,
And those two share the weight and drag the plough,
So, treading as thy Master's steps allow,
No more shall prick the goad by pride provoked.

Aye, pride, perverse, the unwilling shoulder jerks;
But take My yoke on thee and learn of Me,
And thou shalt rest in My humility,
And, going in My strength, shalt do My works.

And, ah, My children, easy shall ye go
Delivered from that burthen of your pride,
Content as infant at his mother's side;
Come, learn of Me, for I am meek and low!

XVIII
Restlessness
(The Disciple)

Ah, Lord, we are aweary!
And yet we think on Thee,
On our beds remember Thee;
But comfort fails to come;
Rest keeps not in our home.

We wake in the night watches,
And fear and shame wake too;
Some word we spake ten years since,
A chance the day may bring;—
How shall we rise and sing!

As aspen trees whose leaves be
A thousand little fears!
As fettered Titans burdened
With the ills the world oppress,
Impotent to redress!

No rest for us remaineth?
Yea, sure there is a rest
Where toss'd souls come to anchor;
A place where we be still,
Nor stirs our restless will.

We come to One who knows us;
He lays controlling hand;
Fightings and fears cease from us,
The Rest of God we keep
As child who falls on sleep.

XIX

At the fair
(The Disciple)

EAGER we take our way through noisy mart,
Agog for bargains that shall souls appease,
Shall minister to happiness or ease,
Shall give us courage for our per'lous part,

Or soothe the soreness of our wounded heart!
They cry their tinsel wares nor ever cease;
We buy in hope of joy and wealth's increase;
Brought home, our sorry bargain, stript of art,

Mocks our desire. But in the fair was One
We would not hear, whose cry was only, "Rest":
"Why hither, thither, will ye frenzied run?

"Come, buy, but bring no money; cease your quest
For unguent never made beneath the sun;
Come unto Me, and I will give you rest!"

XX
Happy Ye!

TURNING to the disciples, spake He low
   A word intended for their ear alone;
   For not in all things were the Seventy one
With crowds that gathered as to see a show.

"Bless'd are the eyes," saith Christ, "which see the
     things
   Discovered unto you, graced to perceive;
   Bless'd are your ears, kept open to receive
What had been precious to renowned kings

"And prophets long ago! This word of 'Rest,'
   Had it stood single, the one word I spake,
   What power it holds the uneasy world to make
A place of peace where ills may not molest!

"The world's aware and restless with desire;
   Great kings and prophets long ago had yearned
   To see those things that your eyes have discerned,
To hear those words should quicken as with fire!

"But, hearken; then as now, whoso would see
  The glories of the Kingdom must bring eyes;
  An ear must bring he who for hearing sighs;
Wherefore, I say, My children, happy ye!"

XXI
Who is my neighbour?

THAT lawyer, had he pondered long one day
Ere told he in terse words man's intimate need,
And, scoffing, questioned how he should proceed
To seize that *ignis fatuus*, mocked his way?

The Lord perceived the serious thought that lay
Behind his mockery;—"What is decreed?
How readest thou the law? We are agreed
That there those mandates be men must obey."

Said the man, sincere at heart, "The law is love,
Our entire love to God; to neighbour, kind
Behaviour, seeking not our own above

Another's good." Pleased with his honest mind,
Christ bade him go and do; he, set to prove
His point, cried,—"How shall I my neighbour find?"

XXII
My neighbour

AND, first half-smiling at the word,
(So quick to apprehend), the Lord
Told tale should each man straight convince,
Who is his neighbour, ever since;
Not him he goes with day by day
In common work and common play;
Not who lives next in the same street,
Acquaintance he may frequent meet;
No ties of consanguinity,
No chances of proximity,
Limit the law for him would prove
The strait demands of neighbour-love;
No boundaries of race or creed
Shall nullify a neighbours' need;
His need, the single quality
His neighbourhood shall prove to thee!

"But, Lord, Thou know'st, I have mine own;
To shew me kind to them alone
Is all I can; towards them I fail;
How then the whole wide world prevail
To hold in neighbour-love and serve?"

"Nay, thou dost not the rule observe
Whereby thy neighbour to discern;
See'st one whose need calls thee to turn
Aside and help him, that is he,
The neighbour for thy charity:
Unsparing be thy help and kind,
Consoling to his wounded mind
As to his body's urgent need;
Be neighbour to that one indeed:
Not, 'Who's my neighbour?' idle ask
To prove *thee* neighbour, is thy task."

"What if the man should not deserve
The pains I take his need to serve?
Or scanty eagerness display
My labour with his thanks to pay?
If I abhor his way of life
Or am with all his views at strife?
How love I such a man perverse?"

"The Samaritan, he was averse
To the haughty, dominating Jew?
Had not his people wrongs enow
Done by the supercilious race
To keep on record? How efface
This ages-old hostility
And to the wounded neighbour be?
This good man knew the blessed art
Of how to play a neighbour's part,
To cherish him of alien ways,
Nor look for thanks, reward or praise."

The Good Samaritan

"But, Lord, if danger there should be
That ills he suffers fall on me?
Those robbers might have left the friend
In worse case than he stopped to mend;
Had the man died, how ill it were!"

"Ill hap to thee is not thy care
From any act of neighbour-love
To which thy pitying heart shall move:
Run thou with help at neighbour's call,
Not thine to heed what may befall."

"I would be neighbour, Lord, but see,
I have one more perplexity;
With work to do, a place to fill,
I may not wander at my will:
From east and north, from far and near,
Cries of the needy reach mine ear;
Th' ignorant ask for some to teach,
Th' indigent piteous hands outreach;
Do I run up and down the ways
And spend in acts of help my days,
Distraught, I miss my proper task
And poor my aid to them who ask!"

"My son, hast watched a weaver's loom
To see design of carpet come?
The wrong side of the stuff appears;
Vain you note shuttle's work or shears'
The pattern of the piece to shew;
The threads at random to and fro

Travel space; follow one thread,
A blue speck shews, anon, a red;
For your blue woof you look in vain,
Then, sudden, it appears again;
Did that blue thread its transit know
By chance 'twould seem to come and go;
But, see you, there is a design,
And seeming random throws combine
To make the carpet's perfect glow.

"E'en so, a man may never know
The pattern of the web; his part
In the considered work of art
Is ready to the weaver's hand,
Who throws where he would have that strand;
But there be many threads: for each,
The weaver has his use; impeach
Not Wisdom that the work controls
Of myriad eager, differing souls;
But watch *occasion* for the part
"Tis thine to play; then bring thy art
To play it with thy utmost skill,
With generous love and hearty will:
Remember how this man, My friend,
Succoured his neighbour, nor made end
With present aid, for, to provide
The helpless man he alms supplied;
But taxed not his ingenuous mind
Some others, robbed and hurt, to find:
Wait on occasion; ready be

For all that task assigned to thee;
So shalt thou a true neighbour prove
To some distress'd that need thy love.

"There be that all their days shall spend
Apt succour to My poor to lend;
There be that walk an ordered way
And only now and then find play
For neighbour-love beyond their own;
Yet these do well, e'en though alone
Toward their own household, those at hand,
They strict fulfil their Lord's command:
Thy one concern is—watchful be;
Who serves his neighbour, serveth ME."

<h1 style="text-align:center">XXIII</h1>

At the house of Martha

Now, as they trod that dolorous way
Towards Jerusalem, to meet the end,
They came upon a certain day
To village which should shelter lend,
Dear welcome to most honoured Friend:
Martha made haste Christ to receive,
And for her sister did she send;
For He is here in whom believe
The happy sisters twain who erst did sorely grieve.

Then Martha hastes to make a feast
That worthy of their Lord should prove;
To some distress'd that need thy love.
And May—sure, she might at least
Set out the tables, plan, remove,
Bring silver vessels from above
And spread their fairest napery;—
In dainty cates they'd shew their love!
The anxious hostess could not be
Content to let her sit devout at Jesus' knee.

81

Vex'd Martha, cumbered with these cares
Of busy housewife, makes complaint,—
"Lord, car'st Thou not that she forbears
To help me who am night to faint,
As one must be who, sole, prepares
Supper for guests? Nay, bid her serve;
We two must take our equal shares
In work and leisure; I deserve
That she should think of me, o'erstrained in strength and
    nerve."

With kindly smile the Lord regards
The fussy housewife, apt to fret
E'en while she, generous, awards
Excessive service, and is let
And hindered by her sister—set
On one thing only—diligent
To catch each word as in the net
Of her fond heart: she would prevent
Sweet Mary's serving too, in the way her Master meant!

"Nay, Martha, Martha, quiet thee,
Let thy uneasy heart be still;
Scarce blessed shall thy service be
Whilst thou discernest not My will:
Mary hath known her heart to fill
With My peace; upon quiet ear
Shall drop the words of life; for, see,

Diego Velasquez

Christ in the House of Martha and Mary

One thing is needful; draw thou near—
Thy zealous works be less than words thine ear may
    hear."

And Martha felt the word as oil
Drop soothing on her troubled breast;
'Gan she to know how idle, toil,
How willful all her quick unrest;
Not thus should come to her that *Best*
Which Mary had the wit to seize;
And ear to hear His words address'd—
Behold, the secret of all ease;
For who will hear the Son, that soul the Father sees!

XXIV
Satisfied
(The Disciple)

"I SHALL be satisfied," the Psalmist cried,
And in that word plumbed the uneasy sea
Of man's unrest; how good it were to be,
If only for an hour, quite satisfied!

And what is the great hope that, justified,
He pledges to himself with confident "When"?
When like his God he shall awake, sure, then,
Contented shall he be as happy bride.

"Come, learn of Me, and I will give you rest!"
We hear, and straightway our unquiet heart
Enters green place of peace where none molest;

And, in that quiet, cons the subtle art
Of heavenly portraiture, in sheltered nest,
The while His image doth the Lord impart.

XXV
The Good Part
(The Disciple)

AND what, the better part that Mary chose?
Is it, that sweet affection finds a seat,
Humble and tender, at the Master's feet,
The while her love, a healing balm, o'erflows?

A firmer purpose the mild woman knows;
"A woman's love is scarce an offering meet
Except her labouring mind His sayings sweet
Solicit all their fullness to disclose!"

So Mary sat and heard, with ear intent,
Upgathering words that from the Master fell
For day-long ponderings, intelligent.

Ah, dear disciple, sure with thee 'twas well,
Knowing that He who mind and heart had lent,
Would both to His requirements compel!

BOOK III

Of Prayer and Conflict

XXVI
Our Father

THE Lord was praying in a place; and they,
His followers, who envious heard Him say
To God such words as scarce to closest friend
A man might dare confide, His prayer at end,
Gathered about Him; "Teach us this high art;
We, too, would pour 'fore God our inmost heart!"

And Christ, perceiving well that none had taught
These men to bring to God their mind o'er-
fraught
With cares of this life, in one word revealed
The secret of all prayer, so long concealed:
"Father," He bade them pray; and at the word,
Stirr'd heavenward longings in their breast immured!

"Think first on God; say, 'Hallowed be Thy Name;
Let fire of worship all men's hearts inflame!"
And in large place straightway thy feet are set,
As one who sees where earth and heaven be met;
A son's heart joins the general hymn to raise,
And thy most dear concern I' the Father's praise!

"Lordly, wouldst have dominion where thou go'st?
Then pray, 'Thy kingdom come; in God's great host
Each man who serves bears rule; the shout of a King
Amongst them shall to men dominion bring;
And in His army every several soul
Bears share in the glad service of the whole.

"Not wilful shall he be who serves the King;
Go pray, 'Thy will be done'; thy heart shall sing
O'er Earth's dear pageantry, perceiving there,
Well imaged, how on high the angels fair
Do serve the King, who riseth as the sun
And through the hours His gracious course doth run.

"Consumed with fond desires, come there and pray,
'Our Father, gives us bread for this one day!"
Not personal needs alone shall move thy heart
Give every man in prayer a brother's part;
And thine own heart, insatiate, hungry sea,
Shall of thy Father's fullness plenished be.

"Uneasy art thou still, some cloud of sin
Shuts out the sunshine from thy place within?
Go, tell thy Father; pray Him to 'Forgive'!
He hastes to pardon, bids thee forth to live;
One sole condition doth His love impose,
That thou in meekness shalt forgive thy foes!

"Does fear invade thee still lest heavenly peace
Be boon of but a vanishing release
Pray, 'From temptations keep us'; so thy heart
Rests quiet in a child's protected part,
Who knows his father's care about his path
And in his ways love's sweet assurance hath."

XXVII

The importunate prayer

'Twas to these men as if a word
Of childish make-believe they'd heard;
A little child on staff will go
And thinks he leads an army so;
A boulder, castle he defends,
A blade of grass green magic lends,
And all the world belongs to him
In right of his perceptions dim,
To whom small things as great appear,
And what is not as though it were.

But they, being grown men, quick to see,
Distinguish dreams from things that be,
Now, how shall they themselves deceive
With a child's happy make-believe?
That they should ask, and God should grant
Attention to each petty want
They tell Him of in prayer, why that
Were the child's foolishness, whereat
Grave, thoughtful men could only smile
E'en though they wished it true the while:

Reflect, how many men there be
In all the world; if each were free
The listening ear of God to assail
With tale of wants that never fail,
If God were pledged to grant to each
That blessing most beyond his reach,
And therefore most to be desired,
If men to rule the heavens aspired
By force of importunity,
Why, where were then the Deity?
"God serving at all men's command
Is not the Lord we understand!"

Christ saw the men's perplexity,
The doubts, howe'er unwillingly,
They entertained; nor could He give
To men unready to receive.
The limitations of a man,
He knew, confined in narrow span
Their mortal thought, nor could they gauge
All the word "Infinite" should presage;
Scarce could they the conception reach
That "Infinite God" is God for each,—
At leisure for each man's distress
As though none else prayed Him to bless.

Not ready, they, God's ways to learn,
Nor the Almighty to discern
In ways so tender with each soul
As were his small concerns the whole:—

So, milk for babes, the Lord imparts
In tale, to nourish feeble hearts,
Like ours and theirs.

                "A man would sleep,
And all his family would keep
About him in the private night;
No person might for reason slight
Disturb the slumb'ring family.
'Tis midnight and all silent be,
When instant knock disturbs the peace;
The father lies, hoping 'twill cease,
That constant knocking at the door;
The man outside but knocks the more.
At last the master of the house
Unwillingly himself doth rouse;
A friend's familiar voice he hears;
It is thy neighbour, have no fears;
A friend of mine has in the night
Arrived, and I'm in sorry plight
With nought to set before him; so,
I haste to beg of one I know
Full-willing; now, I pray thee, lend
Three loaves to set before my friend!"

"'Trouble me not,' the neighbour cries;
'Thou wouldst not have me now arise,
Disturb my children, quit my bed,
That this trav'ller, forsooth, be fed?"
"He turns him round and feign to sleep,

But th' other doth incessant keep
Persistent knockings at the door;
Anon, he cries, ' I can no more
Of this incessant knocking stand,
I'll e'en get up, and to his hand
Give the three loaves; but not for love;
My peace I hold my friend above!"

"If God were e'en than man no more,
Persistent knockings at His door,
Persistent crying on His grace,—
Will these not cause Him turn His face?
The man gat up the loaves to lend,
Not, for the other was his friend,
But, for his importunity'
Disturbed the night's tranquility."

"But, Lord, sure God is more than man,
For what He willeth, that He can:
Now God is love and willeth good:
Why then should men's prayers be withstood!"

"Nay, son, thou reasonest well, but think
Again, how men in friendship link
Their hearts and lives; one asks, one gives;
In importunity there lives
Soliciting of love! Remote
Were God indeed if straight He smote
The sinner nor gave power to pray;
If straight He granted, on that day

A man first asked, some blessing sweet
Had brought the suppliant to His feet.
The man takes up the gift He craved;
Evil from which he hath been saved
Is out of mind, now; God is not
In all his thoughts; he hath forgot
Deliverance too lightly won;
And holy intercourse, begun
In hour of peril or desire,
Goes out as a neglected fire.

"Wherefore, your Father bears to hear
Recited in His tireless ear
Again, again, and every day,
Those needs have moved men's hearts to pray:
The day may come when ye, at one
With God who loves you, for love's sake
Shall come to Him with words that break
From out the fullness of a heart
That finds in Him the better part.
But how should men of carnal mood
Else teach their hearts to think of God?"

XXVIII
Supply and Demand

MEN weary their uneasy mind
That they equation fair may find
Between the world's too scant Supply
And the Demand, whose urgent cry
Reverberates ceaseless in the ear
Of him would walk in love and fear.

A new thing, this, they say, and sigh;
The men of old, not theirs to try
To equalize things unequal found,
To make the strait Supply go round,
To still Demand's incessant claim,
Nor work injustice in the name
Of pity, charity and love;
Our times are hard all times above!

How wonderful Thy ways, O Lord,
What strange solutions in Thy Word!
Thou bidd'st Demand come, clamorous, there,
Where the Father sits to answer prayer:
Dost unconditioned charter grant

To whoso comes with urgent want:
Nay, ask and have! It is the law,
If any to God's throne shall draw,
Urging his passionate request,
He's answered by as prompt behest:
"Go," saith the Father to those Powers
Who wait His pleasure through the hours,—
"See ye that man, behold, he prays:
Now look ye to it that his days
Be graced with that he doth demand!
No man craves vainly at My hand;
Who knocks at My door is brought in;
Who grieves him for his heavy sin,
Losing his burden, goes away
Rejoicing in the cheerful day;
Who seeks, scarce knowing how to name
The good he craves, shall find the same;
How were I Father if one child
Of all My offspring, rude or mild,
Should seek in vain His Father's ear
Nor get what thing he asks?"

                 In fear
Of God, in joy of such vast hope,
His hearers' trembling lips dared ope
To cry on Christ:—"Too good the news,
That God will ne'er his boon refuse
To him who asks, believing; say,
Can e'en Almighty God display
Such power, such lavish wealth bestow,

On countless suppliants below?"
"Nay, children, will ye understand
That nothing may that prayer withstand
A child brings to his father's ear;
And are ye not God's children dear?
Nay, even ye know how to give
Those gifts by which your children live;
Who proffers stone or serpent, when
His child asks bread or fish? If, then,
Ye know to give the thing that's good
To your dependent clamorous brood
Tho' ye be evil, ye shall find
God who is Good, your Father kind,
Knows how to grant him all his mind
Who comes in prayer.

       "Shall He not give
His Spirit that His child may live?
For every prayer a man may raise
Asks life, more fulness in his days;—
One answer for all prayers is meet;
The Father sends the Paraclete,
And with His coming is there life,
Fulness of days, surcease of strife:
The Father's single gift contains
Appeasement for all human pains,
For all men's cravings for increase,
For weary sighings after peace;
No good thing that a man requires
But comes with Pentecostal fires;

All 'comfort, life and fire of love'
Descend with the celestial Dove!
Would any man ask more than these,—
Substance, good friends and general ease?
No good thing will your God refuse
To child who his own Father sues."

ALBRECHT DÜRER

"Our Father"

XXIX

He cometh into an house

He entereth an house
To rest from heavy toils;
To break bread with His friends,
The Master brings the Twelve.
Had sudden weakness fallen
On the Source of all our strength?
Was He spent as one of us
By labours He had done?
Had virtue gone from Him
In all the words He taught,
In healings, journeyings?

Would, ours had been the house
Where came the Lord to rest,
To eat and be refreshed
Even as a man fatigued!
How wonderful the Lord,—
A Man, exhausted, faint,
Our God of mighty works!
But Love may not be hid:
The craving people sought

And found where was the Lord;
They would not be repelled,
But surged, a sea of men,
And brake against that house,
Despite those ardent friends
At hand to guard His rest.
Through roof, through doorway, urge
The thronging multitude;
Can they get near to touch,
Can they afar but hear,
Or see that Face benign
In distant radiance beam,
Blessed they, those eager folk,
The Lord God in their midst!

In vain the board is spread,
In vain kind host entreats
That He would eat and rest:
Multitudes, multitudes throng,
O'er bed and board they come;
No place for a man to stand
Is left, and still they surge.

Christ, pitiful, beholds;
His love flows out on them;
Soon, ancle-deep they stand
In the stream which is our Life;
Ah, happy men, who knew
To find the Very God!

XXX

His friends heard it

Now, who are these of mien distraught,
    Pallid with fear, in angry heat
Urging their way to Him they sought,
    Unchecked by claim of reverence, meet
For any Rabbi? "Nay," they cry;
    "Heed not His words! We know him well;
Our father's Son doth law defy
    And scorn the Heads of Israel;
Say we not well, He is possessed?
    A man beside himself behaves
'Gainst the law, nor fears arrest;
    Blasphemeth He? 'Tis that He raves!
Would any judge the man condemn,
    Beside himself, for reckless speech?
His brethren, sisters—think of them
    He draws within the Law's far reach!
See you, my Masters, we're concerned
    To save Him from a traitor's death;
Within the hour, we haply learned
    The priests intend to take His breath
By Israel's, or, by Roman law;

Nay, an ye love Him, let Him go
Hence free, by reason of that flaw
   In judgment, hinders that He know
What things be prudent. Testify
   To the rulers, if ye friendly be,
Ye heard Him speaking recklessly
   Words might condemn Him, sane were He!"

The Lord, spake He a word, or, meek, allowed
These urgent men to dominate the crowd?

XXXI

One possessed with a devil

Now, see you, Armageddon's field is here
In this same house. What stirs the folk to fear?
A sullen, silent man in raging mood,
Scowling and violent, brake through the crowd
And came where Jesus stood; blind eyes of hate
Glared hard on the mild Lord, nor would he 'bate
His murderous wrath, nor, sightless, lower lids
For all the men could do: lo, Jesus bids;
Sudden, the devil goes; the blind eyes see;
The dumb lips speak the Lord's dear clemency:
Poor man, he was released; a gentle soul,
Set free from demoniacal control!

Be there no more the Lord of love t' oppose
Than fearful brethren sore aware of foes,
And the dislodged devil seeking place
Where best to hinder Christ's converting grace?
"Is this the Son of David?" people cried:
But there were those come thither to deride;
From the City journeyed they to track him down,
With subtleties to thwart, in northern town,
    Provincial.

"Good people there, make way;
Let's hear what this Pretender hath to say,
That He makes bold with God's peculiar right,
Constraining devils, giving blind men sight.
Not far to seek, the power by which He wrought;—
What, know ye not, Beelzebub hath caught
The witless ever by this same device:
First, in his toils some soul doth he entice;
Then, bids his devils go, possess the man;
Calls forth another slave, unfolds his plan,
Bids him depart, set free the man possess'd;—
'So men the more shall follow my behest;
What he believes in orders a man's ways,
And these, convinced, shall serve me all their days':
Now, do ye know the secret of His power
Who hath done works before you this same hour."

The fickle crowd lent a too facile ear;—
"The rulers, sure, know best; how shall't appear
Which of the twain is right? We'll offer test;
This Rabbi works good works be it confess'd,
But, be they works of God? Or is it true
The devil for ill ends good works will do?"
Then, turning to the Lord, these men cried out,
(One minute, quick to praise, the next, to flout),
"Rabbi, we know those works done in our midst,
That devils themselves perform the thing thou
    bidd'st;
But, say whence comes this marv'llous power of
    Thine?
Give sign from heaven that we may know't divine!"

XXXII
Consistency

As men in a crowd see backs of those before
But scarce a face at all, nor can they trace
What prospect lies about them, so these men;
But Christ, uplifted, had beneath His eye
The tumultuous thought engaging every man;
The prospect wide-emerging shewed from whence,
However subtly, every thought advanced,
And whither tended. As Joseph, come to tell
His dream to Pharaoh, would Christ now reveal
To these the casual thoughts each entertained—
As guests who should assume the master's place
And rule his house of soul.
          Patient, the Lord
Confutes these wayward men; "How then, "
Saith He,
"Can Satan expel himself? Can any man
Cast himself forth from house or synagogue?
Another, stronger, needs must turn him out,
Or not a foot he stirs. No man can act
Against himself to hinder or compel:
How then, Beelzebub (who compassed hath

All heights and depths to make a man his thrall),
Shall he bid himself go forth and quit the man?
Bethink you, friends,—that kingdom soonest falls,
Not, which is overthrown by hostile State,
Made desolate with war's horrors,—but that land
Split up by faction, torn to shreds by hate,
Where men take arms against their next of kin
And a man kills his brother. Think ye, then,
Beelzebub slackens his rule to let
Those owning his control waste substance thus?
Would he, indeed, his zealous slave allow
To attack another in that fellowship?
Should Satan cast out Satan, then indeed
His kingdom hath an end; he cannot stand,
And earth is freed from monstrous tyranny!
Too wily, he who knows to keep his own;
And, if your sons claim power to exorcise,
Whence, if they have it, is that power? They'll say
If by the power of God I cast out fiends!"

So spake the Lord; and many a whispered word
And crafty glance went round; as caught in net,
They had no word to say: traced they His power
To Satan, what of them who, arrogant,
In solemn guise went muttering magic spells
O'er men possess'd, who thought them sudden cured,
And praised the sorcerer had delivered them?
Christ, noting their confusion, cried aloud;—
"Perceive and know that which hath come to pass;
If by the power of God I can bid forth

A devil, hidden in the winding ways
Of a man's subtle heart—perceive a sign!
The King is among you, come with no array
Of royal pomp and power, no trumpets' blast;
The Kingdom of God is with you!"
                  Fearful, they
Look right and left if so they may discern
By any sign the King they knew was there;
Thus, truth convinced the men.
               "What sign giv'st Thou,
How know we that the Kingdom of God is come?"

"Hear ye a parable, truth in a tale:—
A robber chieftain held his keep secure;
Had he not raised thick walls, and fortified,
And stationed men at loopholes to command
Approaches to his fort, and on the roofs,
With arrows, lance and spear? What cause to fear
Though in his courts, of many a caravan,
The priceless booty—spices, gems and gold?
So he was merry in his eerie tower;
Voluptuous ease and dance and song were his
To share with his following. What's amiss?
Was he not fully armed, and all his force,
Watchful and clad in armour, tho' they played?
These, foolish, thought not of the sighs and groans,
The muleted merchants, stript and sorely mauled,
Had, year by year, a sad procession,
Borne straight to the King's ear.
            Long, spake He nought;

But on a day He said,—'We must go forth;
Arm Thee, My Son; this robber shall not live.
The King's Son, irresistible, goes out,
His troops, with Him. They take him unawares,
That execrable bandit; his towers storm'd,
His forces slain or captured, he must meet
The King's Son, hand to hand: what careth he?
His armour steel-proof, he himself so strong
Ten men could scarce withstand him, what to him
To battle with this Power? He will go down;—
The wretch lies prostrate, pierced, at feet of him
Whose might he had contemned; of armour stript,
Denuded of the spoils piled in his courts,
What, for the caitiff now?
        Ye ask a sign;
Behold the sign; a tale wherein to read
That which has come upon you. See ye to't;
Behold the Stronger, come to spoil your goods
And claim each man's allegiance."

        A man
Came whisp'ring in His ear,—"Master, pray note,
Not we who said malicious things of Thee—
That Thou by Satan's power expellest fiends—
'Twas the rulers, not we simple citizens;
Nothing said we."
        "And therein lies your guilt.
Who is not with Me is against: no place,
No neutral ground is left for him, who waits,
Loves not, nor hates, nor holds to either side;

Who gathers not with Me, he scattereth;
Come, fill your bosom with the enemy's spoils
And wear your Captain's colours!

XXXIII
"He divideth his spoils"
(The disciple)

"What be the spoils, my Lord, thou bidd'st me share?
And I, a coward soul, how shall I dare
An onset on this mighty man prepare?

"The spoils, My Son, they be the souls of men
That, come as fox in the night he captured then,
When they reposed secure in folded pen."

"But what, my Lord, if he should rise in might
And seize on me, so ill prepared to fight,
Prisoning me where there is no chance of flight?"

"Nay, see'st thou not, his armour he has lost
In which he trusted, bought at heavy cost;
He lies supine, deserted of his host;

"His ancient fame holds men in terror still,
And many souls he keeps against their will;
But hasten thou, their good desires fulfill.

"Take thou thy Captain's mandate, "take His sword;
No weapon hath he to resist My word,
Strong to set free all souls that once have heard.

"Return triumphant with men's souls, his spoil;
Redeem those noble arts he wields to foil
God's purposes, who would all these assoil;-

"The song that cheers a man in listless mood,
Things carved and pictured, wrought in stone and
    wood
According to My pattern—these are good."

XXXIV

The unpardonable sin

THE Lord spake:—

"Men sin and then repent them: blackest sin
Is born of sudden yielding, desperate,
As one who gazing from a dizzy height
Makes unexpected plunge, surprising him:
The man who sinned comest to himself again;
Loathes that ill thing he did and hates himself;
Goes crying to his God to put away
This his so great offence;—an ingrate, he,
Ne'er seeing love and life poured out for him
By faithful hearts of friends till one lies dead,
Forgiveness on her lips no more, nor love:
By the corpse-light of Death, he reads his part;
Seeks where to hide his head, and—finds his God!

"That other lies; nay, lies in open day,
And finds himself unsheltered, unconcealed,
A target for men's scornful eyes and speech!
Alone, and shamed with excess of shame,
Lo, in that solitude, One, he perceives,
Who is the Truth; his soul comes home to God,

115

Forgiveness finds he, and goes forth, true man.
"Another grovels filthy in lust's stye;
Debased, debauched and glorying in his shame,
What hope for him? His God's forgiveness yet,
Going forth to unclean places, finds a way;
One day he's sick of self and loathes it all,
This gluttony of vice; he turns him round,—
His God is standing waiting to forgive,
And that poor soul is cleansed.
                                        Another, see,
Has dyed his heart in the red hue of hate,
Nor kept his hands from murder; as he lies
Alone in prison cell shut out from all
The social cheer from which men hail their mates,
He sees it is his sin that barricades.
From speech or touch with men, from prayer to God;
Out of the deep he cries: 'Have pity, Lord!'
An answer comes,—tears and a broken heart;
And it shall be forgiven, that deadly sin;
God turns to the repentant."
                                        "Is no sin
Beyond God's vast forgiveness?"
                                        "There's one sin
Finds no forgiveness now nor evermore;
For, see you, shame and broken hearts invite
The great Physician's healing. Who binds up
The unwounded limb, the arrogant high heart?
There are who see a holy man do works,
Live life reproachless, full of gentle deeds
Which flow from him, in commerce with his God;

One comes; saith he, 'A devil hath done this;
"Tis more than flesh can do, and must be wrought
By him whose hand wields all the strength of hell!"
What for the man who lies, misnames the good,
Proclaims it evil, of the devil born?
For him no pardon is: a bird will perch
On slenderest twig and sing aloud his joy;
Is no twig spread for him, he takes his flight
To place where he can rest: that Dove, divine
Forgiveness, must find place to rest and croon;
The shattered potsherds of a broken heart
Offer fit perch, while smooth complacency
Affords no foothold; so, the easy man
Who sullies with suspicion goodness shewn
By the meek soul and mild, the place of tears
Is not for him; how shall he be forgiven?
The act requireth two; man who repents,
And God who pardons him; the guileful man
Who sees men false, for he is false himself,
Yields no place for forgiveness.
                                 Verily,
All sins that men may do your God forgives,
Though they blaspheme the Father, mock the Son;
But there's a sin forgiveness cannot find;
Who scorns the Holy Ghost, no hope for him,
In this world nor another. 'How,' say ye,
'Shall men blaspheme against the Holy Ghost?
Here is a sin we know not; who's to blame
For the offence unwitting?' Understand;
All love, all goodness, a man manifests,

Is as the light of candle in dark place;
The Spirit shines within him, wherefore he
Emits love, joy and gentleness, perforce;
Now comes a man and rails,—'This goodness, pah,
There's brimstone in its flame,—the devil's torch'!—
See you, that man blasphemes the Holy Ghost
From whom all goodness flows. Behold your fault,
Who said that I cast out by sorcery
The devil from yon wretched man. One task,
One labour, is for every man; to *know*
The good he sees, the truth he hears;—nor dare,
Confounding truth and error, good and ill,
Cry, 'Which is which? How is a man to know?' "

XXXV
The unclean spirit returning

THE man whose spirit had been healed sat still;
"Tis good to be at rest," he thought, "secure."
The Lord was there and spake but could not fill
That void heart with his presence, nor assure
The man 'twas not enough to sit in place
Made clean by Christ, unplenished of His grace.

The spirit dispossessed went through dry ways
Seeking for rest, nor finding what He sought,
But driven here and there; "No more delays,"
Saith he, "I will return whence I came out;
Perchance the Christ is absent, or let's be,
Or the man deliver'd is yet fain for me."

By fear of Christ subdued, not yet he dare
Go single to the place so long his home;
But seven strong spirits woos he, all aware
The King's come to His own; they fain would roam
No further, "Let's try against His, our might;
Though we be beaten, we at least shall fight."

The man, complacent, smiled, and thought to keep
From all unease his soul, that she might sit
In quiet every day; to him, asleep,
Came the eight armed powers; his mother-wit,
He held, would keep him in his order'd life;—
They made his soul the stage of hellish strife.

XXXVI
The empty house
(The disciple)

AH me, we sweep our house and garnish fair;
The tarnish of a sin do we abhor;
Dainty and delicate our place shall be;
Shall we not find our secret solace there
And sit and smile and say, Behold, how fair!
But, ere we set ourself to deck our place,
Was one who held possession of the place;
He was cast out and found not where to dwell,
But roaming desolate bethought him well
Of that good place he had held;—I will return
With seven spirits strong as I and take
That house again and make thereof a hell!

Lord, take my vacant house and dwell therein,
For only where Thou art's no place for sin';
All empty domiciles let devils in!

XXXVII

"Blessed is the womb"

A WOMAN in the crowd lifts up her eyes
And looking on the Lord beholds Him good:
She thought of her who still'd His infant cries,
And gave him from her breast His proper food;
Half-envious, half-adoring, she lifts voice,
"O thou that bar'st and suckledst Him, rejoice!"

The Lord this tender mother-soul regards,
And fain would give her a yet dearer bliss
Than hers she envied so; "there be rewards
Sweeter, good mother, than an infant's kiss;
The Word of God, that Word I speak to thee,
Fulfils that soul, hears in sincerity:

"Come, drink, as thou wert infant at the breast,
The Word, shall nourish thee and make thee grow;
Come, as an infant, drink; none shall molest
The soul that knows from whom its blessings flow;
Rest from thy labours, be as babe once more;
Thy God knows well to nourish and restore!"

XXXVIII
The Sign of Jonah

THE people heard His words and, more and more,
They gathered close that they might nothing lose
Of that they late discerned was their life,—
Aye, more than bread—the Word of God He spake.
Envious, His enemies hung on the crowd,
Devised a trap, a cunning net of words
Should catch Him to His fall.

                      "Master," say they—
A group of Pharisees and scribes, well skilled
In subtle turns of speech which make appeal
To a man's vanity, credulity,—
"With interest we hear Thy teaching new:
But, as Thou know'st, the new must needs be tried;
We, too, be masters in Israel; were't fit
That prophets false and true, how know we which?
Should win our patient ear? Now, be advised;
Thou speak'st of heaven as one who knew the land,
Could summon its resources; do but bid,
And, lo, a sign celestial shall convince
The dullest and most hard."

                        The Master heard,

George Frederic Watts

Jonah

And, as with lightning's flash, instant revealed
Their hearts to those men—sorry sign for them,
Those moral men, of standing in the world!
Their life voluptuous of secret vice,
Few men could know of that, so crafty, they:
"Adulterous generation," cries the Lord,
And sees them wince at the word;—"Ye seek a sign?
A prophet once was bidden to go forth
And preach to men as vile as you, to-day,
Of the Lord's doom on sin; he tarried long,—
The city was a great one,—and, at last,
Took ship to flee God's bidding. Ye all know
The end. As Jonah lay entombed three days
And nights, so shall the Son of Man. 'Who, then,
This Son of Man, is He?' ye scoffing ask:
As he once sent for sign to Nineveh,
Lo, One to you is sent, and ye see not.
Think ye a sign may come and go nor shew
Portent? I tell you, nay; who fails to see
The signal sent shall perish certainly
As ship struck on a rock for lack of care
To note the warning light for safety set
"The men of Nineveh, sinners extreme,
Shall judge you of Jerusalem. One came
And bade, 'Repent, ere righteous vengeance fall!"
The people turned, repentant; sat in dust,
Laid ashes on their head, and God forgave,—
For there were many children in the place.
One, more than Jonah crieth in your ear,—
'O Israel! Behold, your God's at hand,—

Humble yourselves that ye be not cast out,
Your sins upon your heads!' Do ye give ear?
I trow not; ye go far in quest of Me,
Not for your healing, but to take My life;
Ye men of Nineveh, rise up and judge!
Remember ye that Queen, who journeyed far
For that she heard King Solomon was wise,
And words of wisdom knew she for the best
The world contained; so from the ends of the earth
Came she to gather counsel. Fools and blind!
What hinders you to wait on the Oracle
Of God who speaks with you? Consider then,
One greater far than Solomon is here!"

BOOK IV

Of Self-Deception and of Signs

XXXIX
"Woe unto you, Pharisee"

"Rabbi, to dine with me, wilt please?
There, in cool chamber fairly set,
O'er cup of chosen wine, we'll get
Some quiet talk; I fain would know
The novel doctrines Thou dost shew."

One Guest in all the world comes sure
To him who bids, without allure
Of meat or music, costly wine,
Or talk that woos a man to dine.
The Lord went with Him, took His seat
At the table duly laid for meat.

Remembered He an earlier day
When thus a Pharisee did pray
Him and His following to eat,
When the disciples sat at meat
With hands unwashed? The Lord took thought
Nor washed; this negligence was fraught
With sure offence to host whose eye,
Fastidious, was quick to spy

Omission of accustomed rite
In guest whom he deigned to invite,
Scarce knowing Him
                              The Lord discerned
This Pharisee's arrogance; He turned,
Imperial, at the proud man's board,
And spake that awful judgment word,
From which is no reprieve, to those
Assembled there, vain men who chose
To sit in the scorner's seat.
                                    "Without,
Ye Pharisees be clean, no doubt,
In cup and platter, house and hands;
But a clean heart your God demands;
Look well within, and ye shall find
Schemes of extortion fill your mind;
Lying, uncleanness, greed and hate
Are in your heart, while ye abate
No tittle of presumptuous claim
To magnify His holy Name,
The God of Israel. Ye fools,
Who think to please Him with nice rules!
Is God concerned with things outside?
Will He not all your pains deride
Who makes a decent, reverent show
In things external, while ye go
On still in wickedness? Who made
The heart, think you? Who hath displayed
A thousand wiles to win that heart
So eager ever to depart

From God's own ways?

                        Would ye be clean,
Look well to secret places seen
By Him who made you; find ye there
Extortion, lust, oppressing greed?
Give ye an alms to them who need
Of even these,—the widow's tears
Unshed, for timely help appears,
The shame the virgin shall not feel
Because ye have refrained to steal
The flower of her virginity;
Such alms if ye shall bring to Me,
Clean are ye every whit!

                             Your care,—
That, mint and anise pay their share,
Their tenth to God; what would He more?
This, that your judgment shall restore
The poor man's pledge; the rich, undo,
For offences manifest to you:
The love of God shall fervent flow
In hearts constrained that love to shew
To needy brother. Do but this,
And tithes and alms come not amiss
From heart that, like the almond-tree
Puts out fair flowers spontaneously.

"Woe be to you, ye Pharisees!
Remember ye the God who sees
You choose the chief seats in His place,
Where men to worship come; what grace

For him who seeks vain glory there
Where men be met for praise and prayer?

"Woe be to you, ye Pharisees,
Whom all men's salutations please!
Ye walk the market-place in pride,
And no man dares your hate abide,—
All make obeisance,—Woe to you!

"Like tombs are ye, fair to the eye,
All green and flower-bedecked, none spy
The hid corruption underneath,
Nor know they touch the place of death!"

Amazed the guests; none dared reply
Or wag a tongue or move an eye,
But with fixed gaze beheld the Lord
Those men who heard His damning word.

XL

"Woe unto you, ye lawyers"

A LAWYER, bolder than the rest,
Plucked heart to utter flippant jest;—
"Master, Thou wouldst not slight the Law,
But from Thy words we too must draw
Our condemnation; pray remove
Thy blame if Thou wouldst not reprove!"

The wrath of Christ quick on this scoffer fell!
"Ye have judged well in this; Woe unto you,
Ye lawyers, for the burdens that ye lay
On poor men's backs with your, Thou shalt, shalt
    not,—
Laws never laid of God, which weigh on men
Whether they sit or walk, or eat and drink,
Or hide them; there is no escape from you;
Your laws find out the poor soul, bind him down,
While scatheless go ye, nor with finger touch
The burdens ye have laid. Woe unto you.

"Woe unto you, I say! Men's praise ye claim
For costly tomb to ancient prophet raised;

Say ye, "How fair this marble edifice,
How worthy him, Isaiah, Micah, some
Servant of God, sent Israel's sins to chide.

"Poor Israel! Your fathers knew to deal
With men perversely righteous who rebuked
The iniquities of their people. Fire and sword
Offered quick remedy, and some were stoned,
Some, sawn asunder. Well, to-day, do ye
Build sepulchres for men your fathers slew,
And set your seal as to a righteous deed!

"What think ye of God the while? Is't that He sleeps
Nor knows the Apostles sent to preach His Name,
Prophets who sealed their message with their blood?
I tell you, God observeth!
                    Men of laws,
Do ye not know the elements of law,
That crime and never-failing punishment
Follow, the one the other? 'God is slow,'
Say ye, "forgets the blood of prophets shed
From Abel to Zacharias; should He wake,
Here be the tombs we built to placate Him
And do His servants honour.'
                    Fools and blind!
I tell you none before God is forgot,
From righteous Abel, of his brother slain,
To him who fell a martyr as he went
From sanctuary to altar. Ye shall give,
E'en ye, account for all. Believe ye not

That sins of nations pass, or sins of men;
A day of judgment comes; though ages since
The deed was done, he bears the penalty
Whose thought accepts the crime, whose ways
    confirm;
Woe to you lawyers, woe without escape,
For ye know not your offence! Who but ye
The key of knowledge hold,—a bounteous feast
At which men should regale with gladdened eyes,
But ye, well bear ye symbol of the key,
Ye shut the door, lock fast, nor enter in,
Nor open to the ravening multitude!
What, know ye not two hungers be in man;—
Hunger for bread allayed, then clamours mind
For knowledge which is life; the man is dead
Whose thoughts nor traverse the highways of God
Nor note His dealings with the world of men;
Who hath no ear to hear his people's songs
Nor learneth from old tale of valorous deed,
Nor tragedy of crime and punishment,
Certain and meet; who understandeth not
How marvellous His works who hath made men,
How in remembrance all these should be kept!
What knows he of Orion, the Pleiades,
Or of Behemoth in his vast deep?

"The law delivered to him, what is't more
Than a mechanic bidding void of thought
To call up answering thought, to move men's love?
Go to, ye lawyers, empty stores and choked,

Aye, sealed, from which men draw no nutriment
For minds that live by bread! The ignorant,
How know they God, save by His pity taught,
For ye neglect to feed them! Woe to you!"

XLI
The keys of knowledge
(The disciple)

Are, now, no dried-up wells, hermetic seal'd,
As held they water of life? Go we with keys,—
Official proclamation that with these
We could the courts where knowledge is revealed

Ope to the thirsty scholar? Our own ease
Take we the while fair Knowledge lies concealed
'Neath dust of verbiage, nor the fit key yield
To willing learner whom 'tis ours to please?

Believe we then that Knowledge is our own
To give or to refuse, hold or impart,
Or, miser's store, nor use nor give away?

Lord, make us understand terms of that loan
Of gracious Knowledge, of delightsome Art,
For all men's use, Thou lodg'st with us to-day!

XLII

"In perils by mine own countrymen"

THEN left the Lord that cold unkindly house,
That Judas feast at which men would betray
The Lord of life,—men from Jerusalem
To catch Him in His speech sent down. A crowd
Surround the Prince of Peace with clamorous cries,
Rude menacing hands, faces unmeetly thrust
Close to the Face divine, the while they cry,
Tumultuous, vehement,—"What means this,
And this, that Thou hast said? 'tis blasphemy,
Rank blasphemy and treason! Mark our words,
A man's condemned to die for less than this!
Think'st nameless Outcast may thus vilify
The rulers of the people, in the house,
The finely ordered house, of one of us,
Ruler in Israel, and cry fatuous 'Woes'?
Who gave *Thee* authority we fain would know?"

He was alone, remote from all His friends,—
As some fair barque buffeted of the waves,
Torn by the winds,—none of the people there,
Stood Jesus in their midst. And yet, not thus

The Wrath of the Lamb constrained those violent
   men:
Their tongues were free to wag, pour insults sharp
As pointed hailstones wounding tender vine,
But no man dared lay hands on Him;—alone,
He went His way majestic through the storm.
The multitude, drawn thither by the noise,
Found Him again, hidden from them awhile;
Eager they press to hear, the loving crowd;
But know not through what peril He had passed,
Else sudden, "Woe" had fallen upon that house
Wherein Christ was dishonoured.

XLIII
"Bewared of hypocrisy"

Full of the theme forced on Him in that house,
That shameful house, the Lord turned to His own,
And warned the Twelve of sin he must eschew
Who in the Kingdom serves: "Beware," saith He,
"Of leaven the Pharisees do use to raise
Their daily bread, that it be light to eat
And pleasant in the mouth. "What is't?" ask ye:
Hypocrisy, a simulated life
Of show and make-believe, and all for what?
Who is deceived by their so seemly shows?
Not God nor man, I tell you, but themselves;
They live a lie and think the lie they live;
For God hath made men to love righteousness,
So they who are unrighteous make-believe;
Some hide themselves behind long prayers and alms,
As ye have seen a child with hazel wand
Forget his rags and, prideful, strut, a prince.
"The child may make believe and play at kings,
Courts, funerals and goodly festivals,—
He follows but the manner of a child;
A man must put away such childish things,

Nor figure as were he some other one,
Great in good works, deserving all men's praise,
The while his virtue's as a cloak to hide
Foulness and rags within.

                                   A man may not
Act, as a child, 'fore God; his make=believe
Stript sudden from him leaves him shelterless;
Foulness of death within is, bare, displayed
Before men's eyes: then, think not to conceal,
Ye who be My disciples; love and truth
Demand no cov'ring; hide ye pride and greed
'Neath lying rags of holiness, behold,
I strip away the cloak; all men perceive,
And hate the thing they see!

                                   Nor yet shall ye
Make secret allies, whisperers who know all
And, for their own advancement, hide the truth
And join in the game of goodness ye would play;
All a man's words of falsehood and of lust,
Of murderous malice spoken in the ear,—
One from the housetop shall proclaim aloud
That all may hear; nothing is covered up
That shall not be revealed; hid, but is known."

XLIV
"Whom ye shall fear"

THE multitude heard and trembled at the word
Christ spake to His disciples. Woe to them,
Were the Rabbi thus severe! A hundred thefts,
All little matters, scarce to be discerned,
Arose in each man's heart; a hundred lies;
If He condemned the righteous Pharisees,
What hope for common people? Awful fear
Sat heavy on their soul; what if were known
The things they'd done and said, brought in a sum—
Scarce then their lives were from the Ruler's safe

The Lord perceived the thoughts that wrought in
    these;—
They knew the JUDGE was there, the Judgment Day
At hand this very hour, and feared the Lord;
He turned Him round to them; "I say, My friends,"
(E'er tender to these men of small repute!)

"Fear not the rulers who have power to slay,—
What, then, if ye be killed, cast into gaol,
The while ye have God for your friend? Fear Him

142

Whose is that self in you that dieth not,
Your soul,—alive when body is destroyed,
Alive for evermore in weal or woe;
Blissful, if God look on him; if He turn
Away, the poor soul perisheth for lack
Of the life and light of God. Fear God, My friends!

"Say to you, 'We would fear God, but how get bread
In honest ways nor ever lie at all?'
Still say I unto you, Fear God, My friends!
Feedeth He not the sparrows on the roof?
Five buy you for a farthing, and not one's
Forgotten before God; how think ye then
He should forget when sore bestead are ye,
Worth more than many sparrows? Which of you
Hath child so precious he could tell you straight
The number, not of teeth, but of those hairs
His mother combs upon the little head?
But you, your Father numbers every hair!
Fear not, for ye are dear."
                                        "What shall we do?"
Cried the multitude, urged by the love of God:—
And Christ made answer: "God hath sent His Son
For man's salvation: see that ye believe;
The man who shall confess Me before men
Him shall the Son of Man, I say to you,
Confess before the angels; before God,
Shall say, 'This man's My friend who loveth Me.'
But if, for fear of Rulers, one deny,
Say, bold, ' I do not know Him,' to that man,

Atremble in God's presence, Christ shall say,
'I know thee not; thou art no friend of Mine.'

He who denies the truth blasphemeth Him,
The Spirit of all truth, the Holy Ghost;
Speak ill of Christ, and ye shall be forgiven;
But who blasphemes against the Holy Ghost,
Calls truth he knows a lie, the good, calls ill,
For him is no forgiveness.
                         Ye foresee
A day at hand when who confesses Christ
Shall, lonely, be cast out of synagogue,
With never friend or neighbour, next of kin,
Who dare say friendly word, or take his part
'Gainst tyrants that oppress you? Fear ye not;
Nor care what ye shall answer when they ask;
The true shall have the Spirit of all truth
For advocate to answer in your name,
And give you words to utter."

XLV
"Who made Me a judge?"

A MAN stood there who knew the JUDGE at hand,
He, also, though his mean concern was all
For his advantage. "Master," then spake he,
From hot resentful soul, "our father's dead,
My brother hath seized on all belonged to him;
A word from Thee shall serve; bid him, I pray.
That he divide th' inheritance with me."

The listening crowd knew that the man spake truth,
Made sure their RABBI, wise, would intervene,
And right a crying wrong. Christ taught two truths
Better than all inheritance of wealth,
And lasting through the ages. "Man," He said,
"Who made Me judge or divider over you?
If an estate's in dispute, there is the law
And the appointed judges; bid them act;
The powers that be, they are ordained of God?
Consider, what is this inheritance
The thought of which consumes thee with unrest?
A little land, a house, some furnishings—
Small price be these would a man sell his soul!
But ye shall keep your soul a holy place
Where goeth out and in the Lord your God!"

XLVI
Possessions

WHAT are possessions that ye overprize
But make-believe of life, that on yourselves
Ye practise, diligent? Pharisees, all,
While ye believe wealth, possessions,
Have any part in your life, make glad or sad
The heart of man: Ye fools and dull of soul,
Your mind makes its own values; think things dross,
And straight they dross become: a pebble, see,
Is cheap or precious as ye think it so;
Sit loose to your possessions; fix your love
On things eternal; he who thirsts for God
Hath chosen riches that shall cleave to him
In this world and another; he hath life,—
The one possession proper to a man.
Take heed, I bid you, see ye covet not!

XLVII
The rich fool

A CERTAIN farmer laboured hard;
The generous earth gave due reward;
Up early and so late to rest,
Wily in bargaining for the best,
Wary and pinching in his ways,
Hard master, niggardly of praise,
But always there to see that none
Should slack his work for heat of noon;
Early, the furrows long and straight
Spake husbandry on his estate;
The thorny places, stony ground,
To give some yield of corn were bound;
His pastures green, his meadows lush,
His trees, fruit-laden every bush,
Spake praise of this so prosperous man.

Who saw his labourers, began
To doubt if all were well indeed,
Or was his care the care of greed:
Suspicious, hard, the master went;
The men, in sullen discontent

Nor prosperous, nor amply fed,
With downcast eye and heavy tread,
Worked dogged under that sharp eye
So ready every halt to spy.

The man himself worked hard, you say,
A labourer without pause or pay?
Aye, but, was ever in his thought
The day when, his good fortune wrought,
Under his fig-tree, at his ease,
He should be free himself to please;
Should slumber when he had a mind,
Should delicately eat, nor find
His fruits cloy on him; merry, too,
Should wax on wine from grapes he grew.
And oft in his spare-living days
He chuckled as his inward gaze
Fat and well-liking saw himself
Take silver beaker from the shelf
And pour him wine, a brimming cup;
But no poor man did he take up
In all his visions; comfort lent
To never hungering soul, but spent—
"My fruits," "my stores," "my wine," "my pelf"—
All his possessions, on himself.

The wished-for day at last arrives,
(As comes it into most men's lives.)
The harvest yields such bounteous store,
His barns, sure, will contain no more:

He gazes round with inward glee
On signs of his prosperity:
He has attained, and, prudent man,
He realizes while he can:
Not his to labour for increase
With all this plenty; he will cease.

But a perplexity appears;
Not yet have come the happy years;
His barns o'erflow, his house no more
Can hold his too abundant store;
One more great labour; then, the rest,
Compunctions, cares, shall ne'er molest!
"My barns will I pull down," saith he,
"And those I build so vast shall be
That I shall never fret me more
Nor labour: then, my soul, I'll sing,
Happy and careless as a king,—
'Soul, take thine ease, and eat and drink;
Be merry all thy days, nor think
With anxious care of any morrow,
Free, henceforth, from all care and sorrow!'"

(Poor man, his soul he little knew!
What was't to her, the wealth he drew
Together with such eager care?
She might not his possessions share;
How should she eat with him or drink?
Her part to feel, to know, to think!
In solitude the rich man sate,

His sickly soul, disconsolate!)
Sudden, a Call disturbs the man,
At ease according to his plan:
The voice of God proclaims, "Thou fool,
Who plannedst life by thine own rule,
This night thy soul's required of thee;
Then, whose shall thy possessions be?
Nought hast which thou canst take away,
Hast nought laid up for this great day;
Naked, ashamed, thou tak'st thy way
To God's high Presence."
                    See, the fate
Of the man who gathers great estate
But is not rich towards God!

XLVIII
"Be not anxious"

FRET not for feeble days
    Nor any care of life,—
For doubtings and delays,
    For failure, loss or strife.

The life is more than meat,
    The body, than its dress;
Why fret for that ye eat,
    Why let your garb distress?

The ravens neither sow
    Nor gather any store;
God feeds the famished crow,
    Are ye not then much more?

Your fretting brings no gains;
    Ye may not grow a foot
For night-long anxious pains;
    To what doth fretting boot?

If such a little thing
　　As growing in a night
For your accomplishing
　　Forbidden is outright,

Why vex you for the rest,
　　Nor quiet troubled heart,—
"My Father knoweth best;
　　He setteth all my part."

How do the lilies grow
　　In beauty all arrayed,
Not Solomon could shew
　　Himself so fair displayed!

If God thus decorate
　　The grass, so soon to die,
His care, will He abate
　　His child to beautify?

Let Gentiles cry for food,
　　For vesture of delight:
Yours is the higher good,
　　More fair shall ye be dight;

Doth God not know your need?
　　These things He gives to all;
The Kingdom is your meed
　　Who on the Father call:

Go, sell your little wealth,
  Give what ye have away;
And none shall take by stealth
  That good ye choose to-day!

XLIX

The watchful servants

PERCHANCE, a radiant company,
A bridegroom and his friends went by,
Felicitous guests, to bridal feast
They took their way with joyous haste.

And all that crowd who heard the Lord,
Intent on gathering His word,
Turned head to see the cavalcade
Nor thought of words they thus delayed:
But He was gracious, let their mood
Help and not hinder them of good.

He caught their thought and turned it straight
To men at home their lord who wait;—
Servants, whose office was to watch,
Alert the great doors to unlatch
What time they hear the bugle-note
Their lord's home-coming shall denote:
To watch, an easy task, ye say,
What easier than let in, I pray,
The lord of th' house without delay?

But, see you, they had feasted long;
With wine and wassail, lute and song,
They, too, had kept the nuptial feast
As wedding guests, and not the least:
Those servants who have eat and drunk
In heavy lethargy are sunk;
And as the night creeps slowly on,
The first watch, second watch, anon,
The third watch from the temple blows,—
Small marvel they should sleepy, doze,
Without a master's eye and hand
Reminding them of just command.

But there were these, some two or three
In all that drowsy company,
Bethought them of their lord's high grace
And longed to see his glorious face;
Wherefore, alert were they to hear,
And ready when his band drew near;
Scarce had the knocking at the ward
Begun, ere they admit their lord
The lord looks round, and all the tale
Is spread before him; what avail
For lazy ingrates to excuse
Themselves that they had dared abuse
Their master's generous clemency?

Behold, a singular grace did he
To watchful servants, who had loved
Their lord's appearing, nor had roved

In paths of gluttony and ease,
But took fond thought their lord to please:

At table spread for his return
Where flowers are bright and candles burn,
He set these servants in high place
And turned on them a smiling face:
Nay, what is this, —himself he girds,
In spite of their protesting words,
And serves with his own noble hands
Those men had walked in his commands.

How blest those servants, know to wait,
Be their lord's coming soon or late!

L

The thief in the night

Again the Master oped His lips and spake—
So careful lest His servants should mistake
Needful delays for His forgetfulness,
And think, not His the power to blame or bless.
"Watch," said He once again, "your peril lies
In letting summons take you by surprise"
But, for He knew advice of slight avail,
Again He clothed His warning in a tale:—

> "A man had heard of burglaries
> In neighbours' houses; ill at ease,
> He said to this one, that, 'I pray,
> Heaven send those thieves come not my way!"
> And then he went to bed and slept
> Nor ward over his substance kept.
> Peaceful at first the hours wore on;
> But stealthy steps were heard anon,
> Or had been heard did any watch,
> Did any wake, the thieves to catch!
> When morning came, his rifled store
> Vexed the good man each hour the more,

The more his losses he perceived;
'Ah, had I known,' said he, much grieved,
'What hour the thieves would come, awake,
And ready, I, those thieves to take!'

"So be ye ready in that hour
The Son of Man shall come with power."

LI

"Lord, is this word for us?"

THE Disciples held themselves as scholars meek
Waiting on words their Lord should please to speak,
And pondered secretly, each in his heart,—
Was it for them, indeed, this "watcher's" part,—
Vigilant always in their house of soul,
They whose high part it was to teach the whole
Of that deep doctrine Christ to them revealed,
His servants, who their fealty had sealed
By leaving all for Him? As for the rest,
The crowd that went and came, for them 'twere best
That they keep diligent watch lest all they lose
Of words they take not to them, nor refuse,
But careless let them lie.
                         There is no place
In that Republic disciplined by Grace
For privileged class above the general law:
But the Great Teacher doth His scholars draw
By easy lessons, sparing reprimand:
When Peter voiced the rest in meek demand,—
"Lord, is this word for us, or e'en for all?"
Christ straight set forth the law should him enthral
Whose part it is to teach the Word.

LII
The faithful steward

The Lord: -

"Aye, ye be stewards set to deal out meat
With liberal hand and just—that all may eat—
To your Lord's servants; stores have ye to spare
That every labouring hind may get his share;
But wise and faithful shall My steward be,
Not scattering rashly for mere revelry,
But watchful that who eats shall labour, too,
That every man shall his own task pursue,
Fed on that meat, shall for his part sustain—
Be his to toil in work or bear in pain.

"Not for reward he labours, but not slow
His Master, ample bounty to bestow
That day he comes, unlook'd for: he who spent
With liberal hand those goods his Master lent,
Behold, the whole of heaven's unbounded store
Is placed at his disposal; would he more?
Of all the treasures of the potent Word
Is he made steward by his generous Lord;

All ministries of joy and love and peace,
Longsuffering and kindness, soul's release
From sin's sore burthen,—all are in his hand
Who shews him faithful to his Lord's command;
His life, a spring of health and healing, flows,
And blessings mark the path by which he goes.

"But doth My steward lose his faith and cry,
'My Lord delays His coming, what know I?'
And, for he doubts his Master, dare assume
Unrighteous lordship, aye, and doth presume
To lay commands he never heard of Me,
And busy him in envious rivalry,
Forgetting Me to seek for place and power,
Lordly and arrogant,—lo, in an hour
When he's at ease nor thinks at all of Me
I come and summon him.
                              Nor can he see
When judgment overtakes him all he wrought
Nor all the ill his treachery hath brought;
He's torn asunder with divided heart,
And with the unbelieving finds his part!"

LIII
Knowledge and responsibility

THINK ye that knowledge is a little thing
A man may hide away in casket sure,
Certain its worth and beauty shall endure,
Nor, like a timid bird, take sudden wing?

Think ye that none against you count may bring
For that ye know, for 'tis your very own?
I tell you that your knowledge is a loan
For all men's use; ye shall not hide, nor fling

Into the dustbin of your memory,
That knowledge ye with pains have got of Me;
Who knows and teaches not shall feel the sting

Of guilt intolerable when before
The Judge he stands: for him, hath little lore,
A lighter chastisement decrees the King

He that hath much must needs impart the more,
And each shall give according to his store.

LIV
"How am I straitened!"

WHILE the Disciples pondered, with fixed gaze
Upon the Master's countenance, a change
Arrested them; the aspect sweet they knew,
OF their beloved Teacher, passed; in place,
A prophet's gaze, far-seeing, pained, constrained,
Aloof from present, held by things to come,
Met the bewilder'd men, whose tim'rous heart
Froze at a terror not perceived of them.
Then spake the Lord, in accents how remote:—

"A burden's laid on Me! The men I love,
Who go their easy way in careless peace,
Lo, I behold them in consuming flames!
And who hath cast the brand? I, even I,
Bring burnings to Mine own! Consider her,
The mother who regards her suffering babe,
How glad she'd bear his pain! And would not I
Endure pangs as of fire that I might save?

"It may not be; through fire they needs must come,
And what will I an't be already lit?

Searchings of fire shall try My servant's heart—
Is he indeed fulfilling all his part?—
The fire of hate enkindled shall consume
All common joys of life, yea, life itself
For them called by My Name! These things bring I
On them who love Me, have left all for Me!
Think ye I come to shed My peace on earth?
I tell you, nay: division's curse shall fall
On every household where My Name is named:
Be five souls in a house? See them take sides,
Two are for Me, and three be sore against,
Three be for Me, and two afflict the three;
And never hour but, as it drags, dispute
And sick contention wear the spirit out.
Think ye that mother's love must daughter prize?
I tell you, nay; mother her daughter hates,
Daughter against her mother needs must rise
For My sake and the Gospel's. Sire and son
No more of one accord take pleasant way;
There is, the son more than his father loves,
There is, the zealous father shall hold fast
More than the son of his loins; behold, they strive:
And I—this is My doing! Where was peace,
The sword and conflagrations come of Me!
Behold the baptism I must needs go through
In them that love Me!"
                      These words so dreadful
Fall on their hearts as drops of molten lead
From the dear lips of Christ: what think the men?
Will they, too, go away and save themselves?

With shrinking heart see they the perilous state
Of them that follow Christ? They loved the Lord;
And he who loves fears not his own distress
Nor takes precautions for his own estate:
His thoughts fly forth to shield his well-beloved,—
A panoply about the dear one's head,
What recks he if the arrow smites himself?
So they who loved the Lord shrank from that pain,
The hot baptism of fire which should befall
Him—more to each than his own soul or sense!
Wherefore, no terror did Christ's words convey,
But quicken'd love the more. Did Jesus see
Love in their eyes, and was He thereby cheered?

LV
Weather Signs

CHRIST turned Him to the multitude, agape,
Ready to hear His words but heeding not,
And scarce aware when aught is said, which should
Constrain to quick response, decisive act:
"Ye, too, be hypocrites, ye foolish ones,
Playing at life the while ye read the signs
Displayed above, foretell or wet or fine,
But take no heed of signs more ominous
Enacted in your midst, nor pause to ask
Amid the play of cares ye call your life,—
'Why, here is a new thing, what meaneth it?
What message hath this Prophet in our midst?
Denote His words fair weather, or more foul
Than this cloud-heavy day we labour in?
What is't to us, what comes? Our Rulers, sure,
'Tis theirs to know the portent and declare;
We have our bread to get!' Poor souls, know ye,
There be things more than bread! To read the signs—
Here is the task for each. Think not to play
At heavy toil of getting meat and drink
As if life were but these, nor hope to leave
Your thinking to some wise one while ye work;

This, too, is laid on you,—ye shall discern
For yourselves signs that appear; e'en ye shall judge
How circumstance affects the soul of man!

"Bethink you how ye stand; a man in debt,
His poor estate all mortgaged, lies awake
Pond'ring how best he may propitiate
The adversary who hails him to the judge:
'Nay,' saith he 'I will cry aloud and plead,
Pray him take pity on my wife and babes,
Beg his forgiveness that I took that debt
Upon me I could not discharge'; but, 'Pray,'
(So plans the man, rehearsing all the scene),
'Forgive me, trust me that my arduous days,
The labours of my hands, in part shall pay
This so great debt I owe thee'
                So he pleads,
This poor man with his adversary, knows,
The law set moving once, escape is none,
The judge delivers to the officer
Who casts him into prison, there to lie
Till the last coin be paid! And how to pay
The while he lies inert, a prisoner bound!

"This debtor, in his generation wise,
Knows his sole hope's his adversary to win.
What think ye of him, deep in debt to God,
Who comes not meek to sue to Him he owes
For a reprieve, for pardon; nor discerns
When God sends Messenger to deal with him?"

LVI
"Those Galileans"

Ah, happy men, to walk with One who knows,
To question Him of things that vex the soul,
To ask,—If penalties, beyond control
Of a man's wit and judgment, be for those

Who have displeased the Lord who rules the whole?
"Those Galileans, surely, their fate shews
Them sinners more than most?" Will Christ, the roll
Of God's decrees to curious men, disclose:

'Twere a sad world might neighbours estimate
A man's offences by his griefs and pains,
Might measure by afflictions he sustains
How God doth every man's transgressions rate!

"Nay," saith the Lord, "what are ye more than they?
Would ye escape their fate, repent and pray!"

LVII

The barren fig-tree

DID fearful thought subdue the restless crowd
Of Throne for judgment set? Through words,
not loud
But piercing, penetrating flesh and bone,
Knew they God was at hand? Did sudden moan
Of men oppressed with guilt rise on the air,—
"Spare us, good Lord," cried they, "Thy people
    spare!"?

And what the Word such quick conviction wrought?
Of vineyard spake He; straight their eager thought
Recalled the tale of how the Well-beloved
Planted a vineyard in a place approved,
A very fruitful hill; the choicest vine
He planted there that it should yield good wine;

Nay, more; rude thieves to scare, He built a tower,
And made a winepress, sheltered in a bower;
The vintage time arrived, for grapes He sought
The men who gathered for Him wild grapes brought
Yielding no wine fit for the Master's use,
But draught so sour, the thirsty must refuse.

Then they bethought them how the Lord made haste
That vineyard so unfruitful to lay waste
Remembered how 'twas Israel's tale was told
In figure of that thankless garden, cold
'Neath the warm sunshine of God's fost'ring grace,
Nor yielding grapes to justify its place.

"But, hark, a barren fig-tree is His theme,
Not that curst vineyard of our idle dream;
A fig-tree in the vineyard—what is it?
Belike those Rulers who o'er Israel sit;
The owner looked for fruit among the leaves—
Means He that virtuous semblance men deceives?

"'Three years, I come,' doth this mean, since three
     years
This Rabbi in our common ways appears?
Is He in sooth the Lord, come to demand
That fruit we should deliver to His hand?
And what have we to yield Him? Nought, I trow
Rulers nor people, have we good to shew—

"A rotten race, predestined to our fall!
The gardener hastes him at his Master's call,—
'Cut down this fig-tree cumbering the ground!'
Nay,' saith the Man, 'if I have favour found,
Spare it a year that I may dig and prune,
Then, if it bear not, let its fall be soon!'

"What meaneth He? Have we a spell of grace
Good fruit to yield an we would keep our place?"

LVIII

"A spirit of infirmity"

A SPIRIT of infirmity! Ah, me,
Who may the woman's broken spirit see,
As there in synagogue she takes her place
On Sabbath days, if haply she may trace,
Through ritual of reading, prayer and praise,
Some sign that God remembereth her days?

Men see the poor soul creep, together bent,
Nor care that body to the spirit lent
Its downcast attitude, its springless gait,
Its deep depression nothing can elate;
With loathing pity they the wretch pass by,
Nor the poor prisoned soul within descry.

Then enters ONE who sees and knows the whole,
The long confinement of the fettered soul
Held eighteen years within that painful cage,
In secret suffering that He could gauge
Who knows how flesh upon the spirit preys,
And gives complexion to the leaden days

"Daughter of Abraham," she! And Jesus knew,
Through her long bondage, how her spirit true
Had sought her fathers' God; no alien she:
Her crooked body, He bids straightened be:
Sudden, she stands erect,—ah, glad susrprise!—
A marvel in the Jews' unfriendly eyes:

No longer pressed to earth, her spirit leaps
Beyond her body's state; she Sabbath keeps,
She, also, with a song of joyful praise,
To Him who knows oppressed fold to raise!
The jealous Jews regard with envious eye
The wonder that their hate might not deny;—

They turned them to the people—nor dared chide
Him, who for th' infirm woman had defied
Their niggard reading of God's liberal law;
"There be six days," say they, "in which to draw
To Him for healing, whom ye choose instead
Of Abraham's God who hath our fathers led!"

Their futile wrath they on the people spent,
Nor blamed they Christ for whom their rage was
    meant!
But He, no subterfuge will He allow;
With each of us He deals, as "Thou," and "Thou";
"Ye hypocrites, who each will break the law
As his own interests or pleasure draw,

"How dare ye simulate a righteous wrath
That she, afflicted child of Abraham, hath
Been loosed from bondage on this Sabbath day,
Come to her Father's house to praise and pray?
Whom Satan binds, be they not more to you
Than ox or ass whose bonds ye fain undo?"

What manifestings of the love Divine,
Escaping from the tale, upon us shine!
How good to know the infirmities we bear
In the Eternal Pity have due share;
That bondage of the flesh He comprehends,
And how the spirit fain its bonds transcends;

That, children of Abraham's God, we yet remain
Tho' many years of slavery enchain;
That, straight, the struggling soul from bonds set free
Will rise to where the blessed spirits be,—
The house of God, the place of praise and prayer,
Where joyful breathes she her own native air!

And all the multitude rejoiced to see
This infirm woman set at liberty
From bonds had held her nigh a score of years:—
"What shall Messias do when he appears
Greater, more gracious, than this Man hath
    wrought—
Reducing all His adversaries to nought?"

LIX

On the way

STEADFAST, the Lord with the Twelve pursued His
    way;
Towards Jerusalem he journeyed, pausing not
Nor hasting; as one due at given hour
To meet his friends at genial festival
And slacking pace lest he arrive too soon,—
So went the Lord, due at that Festival—
The Marriage of the Lamb; by slow degrees
Through cities, villages, Peraean wilds,
The sad procession journeyed.

                As they went,
Tremendous issues pressed on Him who knew;
A Man of sorrowful aspect trod the ways
And the people wondered at Him: when He came
To village, city, on His dolorous way,
And the folk gathered eager—for His fame
Was in men's mouths—there spread He feast and
    bade
Them eat of that new bread, the words He spake:

Then, sorrowful and very heavy, passed.
At intervals, one of the Twelve raised voice
And put a case, in part to divert the Lord,
In part to clear his mind, just concepts shape.
Men know, and will not know, when the hour draws
    nigh
For the departure of a dying friend;
So these—long time prepared with chosen words
Tender, solicitous lest sudden shock
Of sorrow break on them whom Jesus loved—
At last, were full aware; calamity,
Immeasurable, awful, imminent,
A precipice with never ledge to scale,
Fronted the fearful men: this thing they knew, —
Bereft of Teacher, Guide, compassionate Friend,
Master and Lord in one, soon should they go,
Foolish and ignorant as they knew themselves,
To teach words held in trust—with none to ask!

So, laboured they to marshal heavy thoughts,
And, as one snatches up a trinket here,
A bauble there, to save from general wreck,
So fetched they up some question from the vast
Confusion of their ignorant forecast.

"Lord, are there few be saved?" one asks, assured
That in the kingdom he has ta'en his place,
As one full early come to see a play:
Situation hazardous the Lord displays

Of him that would be saved;—no certain place,
Continual urging through a narrow way,
And, would one sit at ease, relax himself,
He is of those who seek to enter in
And are not able—frustrate souls and shamed!

LX

"The doors were shut"

THEN, turning to the people, spake the Lord,—
In ready image clothed portentous word:
Of one who made a feast, the tale He told;
In time his doors were shut; late comers bold
Knocked loudly to proclaim them there by right;
Enter they must; did not the Lord invite?

They stand without and raise disturbing din,—
Surely the Lord will bid them enter in!
Familiar, cry they, "Open, Lord, to us!
Thou wouldst not have Thy friends neglected thus!"
But shame awaits them, bold, importunate,
Who bring their lusty summons there too late.

The Lord makes answer,—"Only for my friends
I spread a supper which none else attends;
For you, I know not whence ye are, nor why
Ye assault My house or on its Master cry!"
Abashed an instant, soon they summon heart
And with a hundred pleas support their part:—

"Why, Lord, we ate and drank where Thou didst sit,
Nay, Thou Thyself didst give us sup and bit!
Sure, day by day Thou walkedst up and down,
Teaching and healing in our very town!
We know Thy garb, Thy voice, the way Thou go'st
To that man's house Thou choosest for Thine
host;—

"Canst say Thou dost not know us when we be
Familiar to Thine eyes?" "Depart from Me,
Sinners in deed and thought, who used no skill
In all your doings to discern My will;
Abide without, where desolate weepings be,
And men gnash teeth in dreadful misery,—

"Seeing a glad procession reach the door,
Innumerous as sands on the sea shore;
And every one a joyous welcome meets,
And honoured guests are led to heavenly seats;
For they indeed are Abraham's righteous seed
Who hear God bid, and by His word proceed:
"See how they come, from west and north and south,
Prophets and teachers, here, from whose blest mouth
Issued the Word; your holy fathers, see,
And multitudes of Gentiles who agree
With Abram,—who the Bidding straight obeyed,
How hard soe'er the service on him laid."

LXI
"That fox"

As the Lord spake, that self-same hour,
   Some Pharisees stood by
To whom news of the court had leaked,
   The King's impatient cry—
"Bring me that Man of Nazareth,
   And ye shall see Him die!"

Go, "Get Thee hence," those friendly men
   (Or were they hidden foes?)
Conjured Him, "for King Herod means
   To end the earthly woes
Of all disturbers of his peace;
   Be not found amongst those!"

The Lord, who knows what is in men
   At the crafty Ruler mocks,
Half smiling, in quick insight says,
   "Go, tell that cunning fox—
Who dreams his word hath might enough
   To move the solid rocks—

"The mountains he perchance may move,
　　But not by kings' decrees
Have come to pass the least events
　　That cause mankind unease;
Though he conceives it is his word
　　That binds a man or frees.

"He threatens, but secure I go;
　　To-morrow and to-day,
I cast out devils, sick men cure,
　　In the accustomed way;
As though for many years 'mongst men
　　I were constrained to stay.

"Have ye observed a dragon fly
　　Break from its dingy case,
And, shaking out the crumpled folds,
　　Rise on its wings of lace?
Thus, on the third day perfected,
　　My Rising men shall grace.

"To-day, the next, the following day,
　　I fulfil the decree;
For, Jerusalem, thou mistress hard,
　　Who killed the prophets, see,
It cannot be, the last of these
　　Shall perish out of thee!"

LXII

Lamentation over Jerusalem

THE Lord lift up His voice and, passionate,
Lamented the loved city, for that fate
He only might perceive, and all the woes
Dreadful, unnameable, to fall on those,
Rejected Him to-day; how would He yet
Have gathered them, rebellious, had they let!

In the garden of God, in Eden hast thou been,
Thou city glorious in the subtle sheen
Of every precious stone! Jasper and gold
Beryl and emerald hast thou used of old
For thine adorning! Thou fill'st up the sum—
Perfect in beauty, to great wisdom come!

Upon the holy mountain of thy God,
Anointed cherub wert thou, ere the rod
Was raised in menace for thy backslidings,
Thy willfulness perverse, thy misguidings;—
But thou wert perfect in thy ways when there
I placed thee, sure, a covering cherub fair!

Thy beauty was too much for thee; thy heart
Forsook the wisdom that became thy part;
In folly thous hast made thyself profane;
In treacherous traffic multiplied thy gain;
Thy sanctuaries are no more kept for Him
Who lodg'd of old between the cherubim.

Saith the Lord God, "Against thee am I turned;
Thy temple overthrown, thy dwellings burned,
To ashes will I bring thee in the sight
Of those who long have named thee their delight;—
Astonished at thee, shall the people be,
And terror overtaketh them who see!

"Jerusalem, Jerusalem, hast stoned
The messengers I sent thee, nor atoned
With tears, in sackcloth, for thy vast offence,
Hast killed My prophets and, harsh, driven hence
My holy men of old, yet do I love
Thy very stones all other things above!

"My prophets have I sent thee, a long line,
Of men whom I had charged with words divine:
What hast thou done to them? Made haste to kill!
And now, with My blood, that red cup wilt fill,
The cup of thine iniquity! I grieve
That thou, how late soe'er, wilt not believe!

"How oft would I have gathered in My love
Thy people, dear to Me all folk above!
As mother hen spreads out her wings to shield
Her scarce fledged brood, nor one of them will yield,
Over thy children would I spread My wings,
But ye would not! Alas, for heavy things

"Shall fall on you; your house left desolate,
On Me then shall ye cry aloud, too late!
Ye shall not see Me till ye learn to say,—
And though it tarry, shall arrive the day,—
'Blessed is He that cometh in God's name—
The Son of Man, whom we have put to shame!'"

LXIII
Our City
(The Disciple)

Fair city of our love,
　　Thy very streets are dear,
Thy pavements and thy pleasaunces
　　Where rich and poor appear!

Thy civic palaces,
　　Thy marts where merchants be;
Thy courts where Justice doth preside,
　　Of swift access, and free!

Thy stately halls, and fair,
　　Where pictures on the walls
Let forth the spirit of a man
　　To the land his soul enthrals!

The Churches, where thy God
　　Is sought by pious souls
The Sabbath chime—all turbulence
　　And traffic's tide controls.

A heritage have I,
    My heart expands at sight
Of the good things prepared in thee
    For city folks' delight!

Well have our fathers done
    To build thee graciously,
A pleasant place beneath the sun
    Men come from far to see;

To make good laws and wise
    All men to keep secure;
And, pitiful, build quiet aisles
    To shelter sick and poor!

Then, has the whole been done?
    Have we no part to fill,
But sit and take at ease the good
    Left by our fathers' will?

If Christ in lowly state
    Should walk thy streets to-day,
Would He not pause to contemplate
    The grace thy stones display?

Would not our fathers' work
    Be dear in His eyes, too,
Who watched them build and blessed their aims
    With strength to carry through?

Our slums and hidden dens,
    What would He say of these?
What are our dealings with His poor,
    With sickness, want, disease?

Our city's luxury,
    Will the just Judge pass by?
The vice that crawls in secret ways,
    How shews it 'neath His eye?

God save us from the doom,
    Jerusalem, passed on thee!
Now, let us pray, "Thy kingdom come!"
    And labour that it be!

LXIV
Dinner on Sabbath

AGAIN, a Pharisee the Lord invites
To eat with Him, between the sacred rites
Distinguishing the Sabbath. All the place
Is filled with those who share the rich man's grace;
His friends were there, or Scribes or Pharisees,
And the disciples of the Lord; with these,
Sick men and poor stood round the rich man's door,
Hoping an alms from his abundant store.
A vessel water-logged, a man diseased
With dropsy, caught the haughty glance displeased
Of the fastidious Pharisees; they looked
At Christ full well assured His pity brooked
No sight of suffering, but brought relief
To a poor soul oppressed with any grief.

They nothing spake, but yet Christ answer made
To query in the hearts which He surveyed;
Those haughty men before Him stood arraigned,
Convicted of the scorn they entertained;
Succinct, direct, the Judge states all the case:
Is't lawful or unlawful to embrace

The means of healing on the Sabbath Day?
Confounded by the searching question, they
In confusion held their peace: had they allowed
His right to heal, full sure the eager crowd
Would spread the news that Jesus kept the law,
And multitudes the more to Him would draw;
Nor yet for very shame dared they deny,
Lest men the hardness of their heart decry.

Silent and shamed they stood, while Jesus called
That heavy, suffering man whose state appalled
Those who looked on him. With a word, He healed,
And bade him go. Merciful, He appealed
Once more to those hard men 'gainst pity, proof,
That they might turn them e'en beneath that roof.

"Conceived not, have ye, that poor man's estate,
In whom the waters rise without abate
Until he perish, drowning! Were your ass
Or your own ox at such a sorry pass,
How would ye haste to draw him from the well
Down which, in Sabbath idleness, he fell!

But never have ye pictured in your thought
This poor man's worse condition, evil fraught!
Go ye and have compassion on your kind;
So shall ye measure the Eternal Mind
More surely than with all your rules minute
For Sabbath Day's observance none dispute!"

LXV

The Judge in presence

Now had that Pharisee been aware
That th' JUDGE of all men would be there,
When dainty meats he spread that day
And bade his friends meet honour pay
To his lavish hospitality,—
Would he have ventured, wonder we,
To add, ingredient to his feast,
The company of ONE, not least
In all men's curious thoughts? He asked;
Christ came; and lo, those men were tasked
With that they thought and that they did;
Proud host, vain guests, were equal chid!

First, saw they truth as in a glass,
That poor man's case being made to pass
Before them as a near concern
From which they might not careless turn:
Forth came the judgment from the Lord
With Whom it rests to give award.

As you and I scarce bear to see
A hungry wretch beg charity
Nor haste to feed, so Christ perceived

Men, of this grace, or that, bereaved, —
His bowels of compassion burned
For him, anhungred; straight He turned,
And ministered, or bread or health
Or that more precious spirit's wealth
He only gives: He marked those men
Asked to the feast; perceived that when
Each chose his seat, he urged and strove
To place himself the rest above;
Pride ruled the guests, and all their care,
Their own importance to declare.

Perchance the kind Lord saw as well
Some grace of heart that yet might dwell
In those proud men; so did not scorn
The guests of their offence to warn
In word so plain that never, sure,
Did child more straight rebuke endure.
"When thou art bidden of a man
To marriage feast, make not thy plan
By might or craft the chiefest place
To take; lest comes a swift disgrace:
How know'st thou but some other one
Greater than thou is fixed upon
To fill that seat? 'Give this man place,
Thou hear'st and art ashamed of face.
But what if thou hadst meek begun,
If when the master's eye had run
Over his guests, to each to assign
The place most fitting him, benign,

He sees thee low, and bids thee high,
Is quick thy merit to espy,
The more that thou in naught proclaim
A worthiness men should acclaim:
'Friend, go up higher,' will he speak
To him who no high place doth seek;
And all the guests are glad to see
The lord of the feast thus honour thee.

Bethink you that the ways of men
Fulfill God's will in this; note, then,
How God the man who boasts brings low;
The humble soul, He raiseth, so
That all men wonder at the state
Of him they had not known for great.
Perceive thou, 'tis no chance award;—
Thou art rebuked of thy Lord,
That day before thy friends thou'rt chid
For offence of pride may not be hid:
Thy Lord's "Well done' falls on thine ear
That day men urge thee to appear
In place of honour all unsought'
God for the humble man takes thought.
Behoves all men to understand
That God retains His high command;
The lofty brow shall be brought low,
The humble shall in honour go,—
Behold the law shall rule your times,
Throughout the ages, in all climes!"

LXVI

The host reproved

NOTED the Lord a smile half-hid
In the host whose guests of Him were chid?
Called he, too, help from Him who gives
Those words by which a man's soul lives?
Straight turned Christ to His host, and spake
That word should teach the man to make
A feast well pleasing in the eyes
Of God:—

    "Would'st thou indeed devise
A dinner or a supper, should
Shew in the sight of God as good?
Ask not thy friends, nor rich men call,
Nor brethren nor relations; all
These can make feast for thee again
In proud delight to entertain:
But would'st thou make a feast, My friend,
Whose recompense shall know no end,
Be reckoned at the Judgment day
Among the debts thy God shall pay?
Go, bid the maimed, the blind and poor,
Let orphans gather at thy door;
Bring in the needy to thy feast;
Thy God is honoured in these, least!"

<h1 style="text-align:center">LXVII</h1>

The Great Supper

Not all Christ's words were wholly lost,
One turned to Him with grave accost,
A man that with Him sat at meat:
"Happy the man who hath his seat
At God's high table, where He deals
To them He loves divinest meals!"
And Christ made answer with a tale
Which shewed what virtue should avail!

"Wouldst know how God doth spread His board
    And chosen guests invite
To His great harvest-supper? See,
    Full many have the right
Of entrance to His happy halls
    On that high festal night.

"For many had been bidden long,
    And lest they should forget,
His servants ran to bring them word,
    That nought these men should let;
To house by house came messengers,—
    At no door gladly met.

"One man, by invitation called,
    Was sorry, he had bought
A pasture field his beasts to graze,—
    See it, he must and ought;
The messenger he sent away
    With poor excuses fraught.

"Another busy man must needs
    Five yoke of oxen prove;
'For if I put it off,' said he,
    'Who shall the dealer move
His bargain to forego should I
    Seek favour from his love?'

"A third man said, 'I cannot come;
    I have a wife just wed,
And who would bid a husband forth
    From nuptial board and bed?
Go, tell thy lord that in my place
    Some other may be fed.'

"The servant came, downcast of mien,
    And told his lord these things:
In anger, he cried, "Nevermore
    Kind invitation brings
These men unto my house! Go forth;'—
    He went as he had wings,—

" 'Go forth to city streets and lanes,
   Bring whom you chance to find,
The halt, the lame, the reprobate,
   The destitute, the blind;
So shall my supper furnished be
   With guests to suit my mind!'

"The servant ran the city through
   And hailed men on their way,—
'My lord doth bid thee eat with him
   At his high feast to-day!'
Some hungry folk right joyful came,
   But many turned away.

"The servant said, 'lord, it is done.
   Yet is there room to spare;'
'Go,' said the lord, 'to highway, hedge,
   To distant hamlets fare,—
Compel those strangers to come in,—
   My good things they shall share;
For none of those first bidden may,
   To come before me, dare.' "

LXVIII

The Call
(The Disciple)

Lord God, how great the mystery!
  Thine own, their Lord refused;
For foolish things compared with Thee,
  Thy wondrous grace abused!
And, lo, Thou turnedst unto those,—
Afflicted souls of many woes
  Thou bidd'st appear before Thee!

To all the people scattered wide
  Thy messengers Thou sendest;
To foolish souls whom men deride
  Thy majesty Thou bendest!
Grant me to do Thy bidding, Lord,
And bear the message of Thy word
  To some who hunger for Thee!

And, Lord, forefend lest trivial cares
  My foolish heart so burden

That I reject Thee unawares
   And lose Thy blessed guerdon;
Lest I should find myself with those,
Thy careless friends become Thy foes,
   When all shall stand before Thee!

"There were Gathered an Innumerable Multitude"

REMBRANDT

LXIX

Counting the cost

GREAT multitudes of eager folk
Now follow Him, whose words evoke
Sweet heavenward shootings of the heart,
The wish to choose the better part:—

"Master, 'tis good to be with Thee!
In Thy still presence, clear, we see
How vain the turmoil of our life
Its greed and envy, care and strife!"

"My friends, ye think, an easy thing
It is, belike, to serve the King;
But, hark, whilst I to you declare
How much for Me ye shall forswear.

"What better can a man than serve
His family, who well deserve—
His father, mother, wife and child—
To find him helpful, loving, mild?

"I say to you, these shall he hate,
Should an occasion raise debate,—
Whose claim to service he shall choose,—
Mine must he yield, and them, refuse!"

"But, Lord, we must needs serve our own!
Thou wouldst not have us live alone,
Aliens to those we hold most dear?
This word of Thine engendereth fear!"

"My children, ye must bear your cross;
Who followeth Me shall suffer loss;
Nor, My disciple can he be,
Who gives not all he hath for Me.

"Grave, the alternative before
Every disciple; loves he more
The things he hath than Me? The cost,
I bid him count, lest both be lost.

"If one of you would build a tower,
Goes he to work that very hour,
Or sits he down the cost to count
And reckon if he hath the amount?

"Else, lays he the foundations, straight;
Anon, the diligent builders wait,
And neighbours laugh and wag the head
O'er tower begun,—nor finished.

"Doth any king go forth to war,
Nor reckon what munitions are
Sufficient to encounter him,
Discerns he on th' horizon's rim?

"If he hath but ten thousand men,
The other, ten and ten again,
He sends an ambassage of peace
To make conditions of release!

"So, ye, my friends, think not to take
My service, unprepared to make
Free sacrifice of lesser gain,
Pain to endure and loss sustain:

"Ye think it well that many should
Be My disciples? Salt is good,
But if the salt no savour hath,
Men cast it on the trodden path:

"Consider, then, what is that salt
The disciple shall keep pure, nor halt
At those renunciations, rise,
Ere salted, he, for sacrifice!"

LXX
The lost sheep

THE doctrine of the Lord was hard;
Not ease and plenty His award,
But perils, loss, and strenuous life,
Uneasy days with dangers rife.
And yet the call to men appealed,—
Strange longings in their hearts revealed;
E'en publicans and sinners press
To learn of this new righteousness.

The Pharisees and scribes, repelled
By singular teaching, now beheld
The city's dregs to Him draw near,
Nay, eat with Him at ease nor fear;
"Like unto like," quoth they, and scoff
At One, knew not to hold them off,
The common people; "Well, we see
The kind of Rabbi this must be!"

Then Jesus told that tender tale
Which should a thousand times prevail
To bring within the Shepherd's keep
Some silly, willful, wandering sheep:

BERNHARD PLOCKHORST

The Good Shephard

"A hundred sheep a shepherd had,
And one of these was willful, bad;—
So when the Shepherd turned away,
He ran agate his pranks to play.

"But ere the sheep were in the fold,
The Shepherd's eye their number told;
Lo, one was missing,—he must leave
The rest, that wanderer to retrieve;
Not carelessly, as one in haste,
He searches all the cavernous waste,
But climbs the crags precipitous,
Descends the ravines perilous,

"Hazards his life for that poor sheep,
Too willful in the flock to keep;
How he retrieved the perishing thing,
Did on his shoulders safely bring,
Need not be told: but, happy, he
Cried to his friends, 'Rejoice with me,
The sheep that I had lost is found,
Come, let the gleeful song go round!'

"My friends, see imaged here the love
Of blessed souls who sing above;
And how the angels shout for mirth
When any erring child of earth
Is folded by the Shepherd, brought
Safe to the haven he scarce had sought:
Not nine and ninety righteous folk
Such joy angelical provoke!"

LXXI
The lost piece of silver

THAT willful, ignorant, men seek a way
Beyond the shepherd's tender care to stray,
The Lord had shewn; and how the Shepherd goes
At hazard of His life to rescue those
Who have not wit their proper good to know
And fatuous, plunge their souls in mortal woe

But there be other souls, without their will
Are sunk in miry ways, begrimed, until,
With radiance tarnished, stamp Divine effaced,
By sedulous searching only are they traced:

"A woman who hath lost one silver piece,
Although nine others hath she, doth not cease
Her diligent search for that, so large a part,
A tenth of all the treasures of her heart!

"The woman cherisheth her single piece,
And shall not God concern Him to release
From loss, defilement, all those souls of His,
Without their will have fallen from heavenly bliss?

The Parable of the Lost Piece of Money

"God seeks unresting for each soul that's lost,
With steadfast purpose, never to be crossed;
And, as the woman's friends rejoiced with her,
He hath His neighbours whose delight is sure;

"O'er every fallen soul for Him retrieved,
The angels gladden them, as erst they grieved
That any should escape the Father's care,
And lie, a precious thing all wasted there!"

LXXII
The Prodigal Son

WE know the tale by heart,—
  The wondrous tale!
The son's unthankful part,
  His pride and bale:
And how came want and shame;
  Fond memories;
Intolerable blame
  In his own eyes!
How recollection dwells
  On the old days,
And every memory swells
  His father's praise!

How, help from fickle friends
  He's fain to ask;
To feed his swine, one sends,
  Repulsive task!
They feed and are at ease,
  The very swine!
How the poor wretch 'twould please
  On husks to dine!

And while the grovelling beasts
    He sees devour,—
"Each hired servant feasts
    At this same hour

In that fair home I left—
    Ingrate as these—
Where Father sits, bereft
    Of joy and ease;
For well I know his love
    Remembers still,
The while I heedless rove
    At my vain will:
Ah, knew he all I felt,
    No more austere,
How would his bowels melt,—
    My Father, dear!

"I will arise and go,
    And at his feet
Confess my shame and woe:—
    'I am not meet
Henceforth to be thy son,
    Now let me be
Of thy hired servants one,
    To work for thee!"
He rose and went his way
    With many a sigh—
"E'en thus and thus I'll say
    When I come nigh."

Return of the Prodigal Son

And lo, his father saw,
   A long way off,
The tardy pilgrim draw
   Towards his roof:
He waited not to hear
   The prodigal's prayer,
But ran, ere he came near,
   Embraced him there,
And cried to those at hand,—
   "Here is my son,
Returned from far-off land!
   Go, haste ye, run,—

"Bring hither the best robe,
   For his hand a ring,
Shoes for his wayworn feet,
   See that ye bring!
The fatted calf, go, kill,
   To-day, we'll feast;
My son is with me still,
   Not last nor least!"
The elder brother heard
   With sudden wrath
His father's generous word;
   Sore envy hath

Possession of his heart:
   "These many years
Have not I ta'en my part,
   Through hopes and fears,

To serve thee in my ways?
    What hast thou done,
What lamb hast slain in praise
    Of faithful son?"
"Nay, son, thou art with me
    Through all thy days;
My wealth is shared with thee,
    Behold, thy praise."

That tender Father ran,
    With eager love,
Ere his poor son began
    His grace to move:—
Ah, what an image, this,
    Poor men to cheat,—
The Father's loving kiss,
    Embraces sweet!
Abashed, my heart declines
    To entertain
The hope it yet divines
    In blissful pain!

Ah, who shall certify
    If heavenly truth
In this sweet story lie,
    Of tender ruth?
Who dares my God impugn
    Of piteous art,
Such tenderness as soon
    Must break my heart?

I have the word of One,
  Alone can know:
The sole begotten Son
  Hath told me so!

LXXIII
Divine forgiveness
(The Disciple)

How vast the firmament! We lift our gaze
And search the heavens for a boundary line;
Stars upon stars confound us; we divine
Innumerous orbs within the glorious maze!

So, would we track th' illimitable rays
Of the Divine Perfections, baffled, we;
Outgazing further than weak eyes may see,
Efforts to focus too much glory daze

Our giddy sense! With what relief we rest
On one great star that dominates the sky!
A three-mooned planet, bright, diffusing light,

Divine Forgiveness glorifies our night—
For wilful souls, for those, neglected, lie,
For them who knew and loved, yet—left the *Best!*

Appendix I

"AMONG pictures of what I may call the contemplative order—I mean those dealing with the 'Discourses of Our Lord'—where we see Christ seated instate among His disciples or confessors, the finest example is a mosaic of the fourth century in the church of Sta Pudenciana at Rome. In this, the inspiration, the arrangement of the figures, their solemn air, the atmosphere of dignity which pervades the whole scene, all remind us of classical antiquity. At the first glance we might take it for a gathering of senators and philosophers discussing some abstruse question of politics or morals. And yet the two holy women offering a crown of victory to our Lord strike a note of purely Christian feeling."

Notes on Art from "The Holy Gospels with
Illustrations from the Old Masters."

Appendix II

"BOTTICELLI'S Fortitude is no match, it may be, for any that are coming. Worn, somewhat; and not a little weary, instead of standing ready for all comers, she is sitting,—apparently in reverie, her fingers playing restlessly and idly—nay, I think—even nervously, about the hilt of her sword.

For her battle is not to begin to-day; nor did it begin yesterday. Many a morn and ever have passed since it began; and now—is this to be the ending day of it? And if this—by what manner of end?

That is what Sandro's Fortituude is thinking, and the playing fingers about the sword-hilt would fain let it fall, if it might be: and yet, how swiftly and gladly will they close on it, when the far-off trumpet blows, which she will hear through all her reverie!"

Mornings in Florence, JOHN RUSKIN

BOOK IV
OF SELF-DECEPTION AND OF SIGNS